D1276465

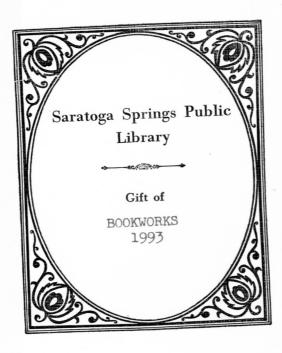

Saratoga Springs Public
Library

Gift of

BOOKWORKS
1993

Also by Douglas Glover

Dog Attempts to Drown Man in Saskatoon

The South Will Rise at Noon

A Guide to Animal Behavior

The Life and Times of Captain N.

The Life and Times of Captain N.

a novel

Douglas Glover

Alfred A. Knopf
New York
1993

This Is a Borzoi Book
Published by Alfred A. Knopf, Inc.

Copyright © 1993 by Douglas Glover

All rights reserved under International and Pan-American Copyright Conventions. Published in the United States by Alfred A. Knopf, Inc., New York. Distributed by Random House, Inc., New York.

Simultaneously published in Canada by McClelland & Stewart Inc., Toronto.

ISBN 0-679-41573-4
LC 92-54474

Manufactured in the United States of America

First Edition

For my son Jacob
that he might know the people
who went before

Canada lies N. N. East from albany
towards the Mississippi.

—Warren Johnson,
Journal, 1761

I am against the future.

—Hendrick "Dutch Henry" Nellis,
The Scourge of Schoharie, 1779

Author's Note

The Life and Times of Captain N. is a work of fiction. Some of the incidents described herein, however, are based loosely on events in the lives of the real Hendrick Nellis; his wife, Priscilla Ramsay; his sons, Robert and William; and Mary Sitts, a white girl Nellis redeemed from the Mississauga in 1787. I have no doubt their descendants and relatives on both sides of the border will find much to complain of.

I wish to acknowledge the following sources: The excerpts from the Iroquois condolence ceremony that appear here and there throughout this book are taken from Horatio Hale's *The Iroquois Book of Rites* (1883). The Mississauga names and songs were translated by A. F. Chamberlain and published in *The Journal of American Folk-Lore* (1888–1890). Oskar's requisition list is an amalgamation of two lists in the Public Archives of Canada, cited in *The Mark of Honour* by Hazel C. Mathews (1965).

The
Life and
Times
of
Captain
N.

The Forbidden Path

August—September 1779

The Water Saint

The boy bears down on his goose quill, splattering dribbles of thin homemade ink on the coiling birch bark. His tongue protrudes and licks his upper lip in his effort of concentration. Are you ready to write? he thinks to himself. Are you ready to tell the truth? Yes.

The boy is fifteen. His father has gone for the King and has disappeared into the forest. His mother has taken to her bed. Her moans and cries drive everyone from the house. In the church his father built in a spare corner of the farm, the villagers say prayers for her and her children and against the boy's father. All the boy's uncles and aunts line up in the pews and denounce their brother. When they have silent prayer, they can hear the boy's mother.

She will not wash or eat. The place smells and fills up with her groans. There are six children besides the boy, who is the oldest. They run wild in the farmyard and in the woods. Neighbors come and help themselves to the farm animals and his father's tools. Thistles and burdock, pigweed and wild mustard choke the corn rows. Deer graze at night where the fences have been breached.

"dear Gen'l Washington, My Father beat us," the boy writes. "He was a terrible Man. We should not be treated badly for what he's done. He beat my Mother & she beat the baby. My Father beat me & I beat Ephas, Jonah, Sophronia, kakaphony & Ella. Then he beat me for beating them & them for letting me. In many ways, he was a Good Man, but you can see why he went to fight for the King. My name is Oskar Nellis. I am a Republican. I think someone ought to return our Cow. Goldie, the Negro, went off with Dad. The other three just ran off into the Forest. They ought to be returned."

The boy stops writing as someone tries the privy latch from the outside. The door swings open to reveal a lean young man in his twenties, long of nose, with a wart on his chin, a dirty slouch hat, and torn knee breeches. He is barefoot, as is Oskar.

This is the water saint, a wandering Dunkard named Tobias Catchpole, who came to pray with Oskar's mother one day three years before, about the time Oskar's father left for the war. She said he brought her the Light. After she got the Light, she stopped talking about Oskar's father. His name was never mentioned. Now Tobias Catchpole has the run of the Nellis place. He has thrown Oskar and Ephas out of their bed in the loft. He kills the chickens and piglets for his dinner without asking permission or sharing with the children. He has sold Oskar's father's clothes to passersby.

"What are you doing?" asks the water saint, letting down his breeches, dropping his pale, dirty haunches over the wooden hole next to Oskar, and squeezing out a long, high-pitched fart.

"Writing," says the boy.

"It's the work of Satan," says the water saint. "Who taught you so?"

"Sir William Johnson's dwarf, sir," Oskar says. "Other children went to the school, but the dwarf taught me to write on birch-bark scrolls before I was old enough for the school."

"Did he teach you to scribe in blood?" the water saint asks.

"No, sir. I have not heard of that method."

"Belike, he was leading you up to it. Did he make you sign any papers?"

"He made me practice signing my name," Oskar says. "But only on birch bark."

"Lord, ye have no doubt signed some devil's pact with the savages. Were there drawings on the scroll?"

"Sometimes."

"We must get thee to water. Lord, we must wash thee in water," says the water saint.

There Was No One

There was no one. Then they were there. They were silent as sunlight.

Granny Hunsacker sat humming in the rocker with her feet on the warming pan. I swear to God she went on humming after Pleasant Wind whacked her on the back of the head and her brains dripped out. She was still humming when he lifted her hair and began trimming the skin round her forehead. When my brother Abiel tried to raise an objection, Approaching Thunder cut him across the stomach with a hunting knife. Abiel sat in Pap's straight-backed chair at the head of the table holding his guts in his shirttail, sniffling. Philomena screamed murder and ran out the door with her skirts over her head. Bird on the Wing and Scattering Light, just boys, no older'n Abiel, tripped her in the pig yard. When she tried to crawl away, they took turns jumping on her till her backbone snapped.

I threw Baby Orvis out the window and dove headfirst after him, and we lit out for the wheat field where Mam and Aunt Annie had been stooking sheaves. The only sounds were Granny Hunsacker humming, Abiel whimpering, and Philomena screaming. But when I looked over my shoulder, Approaching Thunder was standing there watching me run.

I put a half-dozen tree stumps between myself and the house, then made for the nearest stook and burrowed in with Baby Orvis. Philomena was moaning now, muttering, "Mam, Mam—" between moans. I heard Abiel let out one horrible yell. I had not seen hide nor hair of Mam and Aunt Annie, who I figured had struck for the woods as soon as they smelt trouble.

Baby Orvis commenced to crying. I could see by the light filtering through the sheaves he had a goose egg like a blue fist coming out of his forehead where I'd thrown him through the window. I tried to shush him, but it weren't no good. I pulled down the top of my dress and shoved my nipple in his mouth the way I'd seen Mam do, though I hadn't any breasts to speak of, which I reckon Orvis noticed, for he wouldn't take it. Wheat chaff clogged my nose and sifted beneath my dress.

The heat was like a fever.

Outside, everything—the farm buildings, the stumpy fields, the wilderness beyond the fieldstone fence—had grown silent again.

"You are going to get us kilt," I whispered to Baby Orvis. And then I thought, They have kilt my pet dog Romulus.

They kilt Baby Orvis.

Bird on the Wing, wearing Philomena's shift with the seams popped, threw Orvis into the air and caught him on a bayonet about eight or nine times before Orvis quit squalling. I was lying in the wheat stubble with Pleasant Wind standing on my hands. Granny Hunsacker's hair hung from his belt, dripping blood. Orvis's blood arced in the sunlight every time Bird on the Wing heaved him. He tumbled end over end against the blue sky, twisting his head and shrieking, a mangle of blood and blue. Though Orvis had no hair to speak of yet, Bird on the Wing scraped his scalp off and threaded it through a thong on his belt.

We passed Mam and Aunt Annie, lying at the edge of the woods with their limbs flung out and the tops of their heads off and bluebottles buzzing at their open eyes. Grampa Hunsacker was perched unharmed on a rock between their bodies. He sat very straight, with his hands on his knees. When Approaching Thunder beckoned, Grampa Hunsacker stood up and limped over, and Approaching Thunder clubbed him with a musket butt. Then he knelt and sliced off Grampa's hair as though harvesting a cabbage.

The Whirlwind

I have headaches.

The pain begins behind my right eye, radiates across my jaw to my ear, snakes up and fills the vein that stands out on my forehead. When the pain reaches my forehead, my face is suddenly split in two. The right side is on fire, and the left is in shadow. The pain near drives me insane. The savages then must tie me to my horse and lead me. My mind wanders on white-hot wires of pain. Sometimes the only thing that gets me through is to hold one of those sharpish trade knives they call scolpers with the point pressed into the skin of my forehead. Then I imagine drawing the knife down the centerline of my face, splitting the delicate cartilage of my nose, slashing my lips, slicing beneath my chin, then drawing the blade across the underside of my jaw so that I can peel the skin off the right side of my face and release the evils that have lodged there. Riding, bound to my mare, with the knife pressed to my skull, I have drawn blood; I have awakened to find my shirtfront and coat stiff with blood, and blood drying like red earth or paint on the mare's withers.

They say I rave when I am traveling the hot wires, that I speak in a jangle of languages, German, English, and the savage tongues—I know all kinds, and sometimes I feel it is the pressure of all those foreign words that brings on the pain. All those words and the effort to make things fit the words, things for which there are no words.

The forest is a Tower of Babel, and I am a walking Pentecost.

Or I am possessed, as the Dutchers and the savages think, infected by some witch or demon.

Or it is this war and why I am an exile making war on my own people, on my own family.

When I am took with the pain, the savages are afrighted, and, as often as not, they will abandon me after tying me to my horse.

Sometimes they will melt into the forest to prosecute their own evil errands, or they will make for the trails home, especially if they already have scalps and prisoners. Or sometimes, as now, as this day, one or two will make a pact with the others to follow me at some safe distance and wait for the fit to pass to bring me on.

Wabecamegot and Pindigegizig are behind me, out of sight but still connected. The mare follows the path, urged on and made nervous by my moans and muttered imprecations. These savages are Messessageys from beyond the Niagara. They are filthy, credulous, and superstitious—and yet they prefer to follow me above all other in the white man's country.

When the pain comes, it begins with an alteration of my vision; the world is suffused in an aura, a fiery nimbus. Then my eyes begin to sink back into their sockets and the pain throbs into my very soul. Often I puke when the headache starts. I live in two worlds: the world of pain and the world of dream (when I am asleep or unconscious).

The mare stumbles on a creek bank, and I let out a shout.

Across the creek, the forest opens onto a Seneca village with clear fields of female-tended corn as high as your head. To one side of the path, an outcrop of granite looms, angling out, threatening to topple onto unlucky travelers. Upon the rock the savages have painted a face, a huge gloomy face with staring, maniacal eyes and a hatchet nose. The face is split down the middle; half is painted red and half black.

I do not know if it is the face that has frightened the mare or my startled shout. Behind us, the two savages approach on foot, cautiously, for they are always suspicious of Nottaway magic. There is an ancient tribal hatred between these two peoples. But I am startled because I recognize the face; it is the face of my pain.

It is also an image of the False Faces, Seneca deities, servants of the Evil Twin, who have been ordered to serve the people.

The face is meant to ward off the invasion, the army that follows at my back, lumbering unlike any forest creature that has ever taken the Forbidden Path. The Seneca have fled and left their gods. I have seen this before, in every village we have passed. A pole with a dog skin stretched over it and god faces carved on its surface, faces painted on rock.

The Bostonians, as the savages call the Rebels, probe the empty villages with careful scouts, extend their battle lines, unlimber their artillery, and then attack the phantom warriors. They burn the pagods and destroy the False Face images. They burn the green corn and the Indian houses. Then they camp and rest and rejoice in their victory.

Scouts, like the one I lead, haunt the edges of the army, cutting off forage parties, seducing deserters, observing, watching the slow, inexorable destruction of the sacred land.

Beatrice de Holthair

Tobias Catchpole whips the boy in the milk barn where his mother can't hear his screams. The boy does not scream much anyway, as he has grown accustomed to the beatings. His father used to beat him worse. Sometimes his brothers and sisters watch the beatings, taking comfort in seeing Oskar humiliated. It is all the same to Oskar.

Oskar thinks of his father in the forest and almost wishes he had escaped into the trees as well, though he knows he shouldn't. He thinks of Beatrice de Holthair, a Dutch merchant's daughter from Orange, who came with her father one winter day in a sleigh drawn by a pair of black mares. Beatrice was a year or two older than Oskar, with long yellow hair, a round red face, and a plush cape tipped with fur. Stepping down from the sleigh, she slipped and fell in the snow. She snatched up her father's buggy whip and went for the horses, driving them off in a panic. Oskar had to run an hour barefoot to bring them back.

Whack, whack, goes the water saint's belt. Dear Beatrice, thinks Oskar, composing a letter in his head.

"You will not write again," says Catchpole.

"I will not," Oskar says.

"You will have no congress with that evil dwarf Witcacy," says the water saint.

"I will not," says Oskar.

"You will never cross words with your betters again," says Catchpole.

"Definitely not," murmurs Oskar. Dearest Beatrice, he thinks, remembering how his father beat him that day for letting the horses wander (what Beatrice had told him) and delaying their guests' departure.

Twice since, Oskar has spied her riding in her father's delivery cart, accompanied by her older sister and a slope-shouldered youth with a strawberry birthmark spread over half his face like a shadow. Once Beatrice even looked down the hill to the river flats where Oskar was trimming green corn behind the stump fence. She did not seem to recognize him.

The Mohawk boy Tom Wopat tells Oskar that Dutch girls are whores, even the rich ones. Tom Wopat says Beatrice de Holthair is engaged to an elderly Hudson Valley patroon named Weiderpris who has amassed a fortune supplying pitch to the Royal Navy. Tom paints a mental picture of the consummation for Oskar—the bald, carbuncle-nosed Weiderpris dropping his stained half breeches and lifting his linen shirt, Beatrice shrieking with feigned delight, turning to offer the old man a view of her red rump, squealing with the blows of his dried-up palms.

Tom Wopat is always telling Oskar things like this, imaginary things or things Oskar does not trust or does not want to know. Tom is a skinny, tall boy with a tattooed face and body. The sides of his head are shaved; a knotted scalp lock hangs down the back of his neck like a horse's tail. He wears a pair of Oskar's

father's green-glass spectacles, which give him a smug and knowing look, wise beyond his years.

Whack, whack, goes the belt. Oskar bellows. He thinks, he
dreams, My darling Beatrice—

Oskar sits in a split-pine lean-to in a stony stump field high above
the house and the river. The lean-to is meant as a shelter for the
cows in foul weather. The floor inside is muddy, stamped, chopped
by animals' hooves, marked by urine, by cow shit.

There is a late-summer chill in the early morning air. Oskar
squelches his cold toes in a fresh, warm cow flop as he bends over
his birch-bark paper and writes: "Dear Gen'l Washington, You
have not replied to my Last, & since then Things have grown
worse. Gen'l Clinton was through here earlier in the Summer
with his Army & I tried to go for a Soldier but he would not
have me because I am so puny. Actually it was not Gen'l Clinton
himself but a Man named Gimble who worked in the Quartermaster Corpse driving Mules. If you keep a Record of these things
I believe he is lazy & a Drunkard & ill-treats his animals One he
sold to an Indian Squaw died the next Day."

Oskar sucks the end of his goose quill down to a rat tail and
watches Tom Wopat, who squats at the edge of the field, resplendent in his green-glass spectacles, carving a face in a beech tree
with a sharp flint knife. Round about, the forest is black and
dripping. Oskar feels desolate, lonely, cold, and watched. The
forest crouches and smokes like a hot animal, watching him, mysterious and sinister. The forest ate his father. It gobbled him up,
or at least cast a spell making him invisible. What makes Oskar
uncomfortable about the forest is the way it makes everyone who
enters it invisible. The forest is a medium for invisible people.
They disappear forever, or they disappear for a while and pop up
somewhere else or home again. The chilling thing is that for all
Oskar knows his father is standing invisible next to a tree not a
hundred feet away, watching his son dandle his cold feet in the

cooling cow flop. This forest goes a thousand or more miles; Hendrick Nellis had told his son that. It goes up and down the colonies like a curtain, hiding crisscrossing Indian pathways, rivers, lakes, and mountains. It is an immense darkness, a space that extends infinitely within itself.

If his father is watching, Oskar wishes he would show himself. His father has caused enough trouble.

Tom Wopat chops away at his mask, hollowing the tree trunk around it so that the twisted, pouting face, with its outthrust tongue, slowly emerges, white and riffled with flint-knife cuts. There are two dozen such faces staring out of the forest at Oskar, in varying stages of weathering from dead gray to sap white, half-hidden amongst the untouched trees beyond the fence. It makes him shiver to see them. They seem alive, struggling, as it were, to escape the wood out of which they have been carved. Oskar does not understand what the faces signify. Tom Wopat jokes about selling them to the Indians across the river, without telling Oskar what the Indians want them for.

Oskar continues his letter: "My friend Tom Wopat went down to Lake Otsego over the Wagonroad with the Troops & he is no stronger than I only taller by a Foot They did not pay him anyway though he won eight Pounds New York Currency off the Continentals in shooting on the 4th of July. He bought a Pair of Boots & Spurs with the Money. He is half-Savage & covered with Tattoos from Head to Foot but goes around better dressed than me. I am going around to Peter Deygart's who is chairman of the Committee of Public safety & volunteer for the militia. I would be a good Scout on account of I am small & difficult to see. I will also mention my Trouble with T. Catchpole who I believe might be a Tory Sympathizer or a Spy."

Tom Wopat kneels beside Oskar, Tom's shiny boots creaking from newness. He squints downhill at the river through his spectacles.

He says, "Someday there'll be an interstate highway running along the other bank where the castle is now."

"What's an interstate?" Oskar asks.

"I don't know," Tom Wopat says. "An old woman told me."

Scattering Light Nearly Took My Hair

Approaching Thunder ripped my long dress off, and I stood shivering in my shift with my eyes shut, waiting for an ax in the brain. But instead they made me get between Pleasant Wind and Scattering Light, and we went west at a jog trot for an hour till I was about winded. Then the Indians stopped for a rest and a picnic of jerked venison, which they shared with me in equal portions. Approaching Thunder brought me water from a creek in his hat, lent me a pair of moccasins on account of the cut-up condition of my feet, and seemed all in all to be as caring of me as a father.

They were so confident of their escape that presently Approaching Thunder and Pleasant Wind went to sleep while the boys, Scattering Light and Bird on the Wing, took turns firing Grampa's goose gun at the woodpeckers till they'd used up all the powder. They made so much noise that the pursuing horsemen went nigh through the clearing before they noticed the Indians lying about snoring. These were militia boys from Fort Plank, which I knew because one of them, Wubbo Ockels, had flirted with me in July when I took Orvis to the wagon road to watch General Clinton march his troops down from Canjo to Lake Otsego. There were maybe a dozen of them mounted on the sorriest-looking horses, mostly broken-down cart horses full of spavin and quinsy, or ready to drop dead from age. Their officer, all dressed in blue with dirty white facings, let out a yell. And the company tried to halt and regroup. But the officer's plow horse shot straight up the trail without stopping and disappeared.

Wubbo took aim at Approaching Thunder who was sitting up on his elbows trying to get his bearings. But the ball rolled out of his musket muzzle and dropped on the ground before the spark hit the pan. Approaching Thunder just looked at Wubbo dumbfounded. Another shot rang out, and one of the horses went down spouting blood. Pleasant Wind got kicked and broke his collarbone trying to whack a militia man off his horse with the goose gun. So far the horses were doing more destruction than the milly-men.

I tried to pull my shift down over my knees, for I could see by the distraught look on Wubbo's face that he had got the wrong impression of what was going on. He tried to club Approaching Thunder with his musket stock but smashed his horse in the ear instead. The horse reared and went down, probably from sheer exhaustion. Bird on the Wing, still wearing Philomena's clothes, was crawling on all fours hamstringing the horses with a trade knife. Someone grabbed me by the hair and dragged me backward into the underbrush. It was like going underwater, like drowning. The sunlight and air seemed, all at once, to shimmer far above me.

Scattering Light nearly took my hair that first night when he tried to make flat cakes out of a bag of flour he stole from the house, which turned out to be quicklime. The others laughed till they fell off the log they were using. But Scattering Light took it as a personal insult. He made as if to walk into the woods and sulk, then whacked the side of my head from behind with a death maul.

When I come to, he was astraddle my chest slicing into my forehead with a trade knife. I jerked away, which is why I bear a scar like the letter J coming out of my hair.

I missed Mam and Aunt Annie and little Orvis, someone to comfort me through that headache that was like blue lightning flickering inside my skull where Scattering Light had clubbed me. There was some blood as well that made a map of my face.

Approaching Thunder pissed in a handful of dust from his

medicine pouch and made a poultice, which I could barely abide having stuck to my head, it stank so fierce.

Pap was off with Colonel Klock's militia in Clinton's army, fighting Indians, which he could have done just as well if he'd stayed home. I had done most of my missing of him in July when the army went down to Lake Otsego and Wubbo Ockels put his hand up my dress.

This was the kind of war where men got together and marched off to fight Indians, and then Tories and Indians came skulking around, stealing horses and cattle and burning up the place. It was hard on women and farm animals, while the men got to seek safety in numbers and be heroes with artillery. Even if we'd wanted to fight, Pap had only left us the goose gun that took thirty-eight steps to load and was more use as an andiron than an engine of fatality.

But now I was glad he'd been saved, for I prayed he'd come after me one day.

If they let me live that long.

Messages

The forest is alive with messengers and words, false or otherwise, spies, traitors, recruits, deserters, captives, common criminals, hostages, and escaped slaves from Africa who wander around praying to our alien trees (messages unheard).

War is only another species of conversation for us who are in it, an argument, a violent exchange of information. Each man carries his message into the trees, his access to the world of dreams, which others are trying to obliterate. The main effort for any man on the frontier is the effort to understand the messages.

Why am I here? Who is the other? What is he saying?

Those who die are those who do not understand. Those who live understand.

I am for the King, though my wife and the rest of my kin

are against me. I come from a nest of Rebels whom I abhor. Even my children snap at my heels like so many little dogs when I dream. But I have seen a white woman amongst the savages who pleases me dearly. Her name is Alice Kissane, or She Walks the Sky. It is my desire to redeem her from captivity and spawn a more loyal brood after the war.

The others I will burn.

A year ago I gave Goldie, my Negro, to Alice's husband when they came through Catherine's Town. He is a Mingo, a wild Seneca, who dwells in the Ohio country, though he wanders. The Mingo said he would give her up. He said she was a witch anyway. He had seen her one night walking away from him in the woods, breathing fire out of her mouth.

But when I spoke to her, she refused. She would not say why.

I have seen her twice since. Every time we speak, my headaches grow worse. She is beautiful and mad for savages, which many call a sin. She has been too long among them, or she is giving me some message the force of which I cannot comprehend.

The first white child I redeemed was in 1760 after Sir William Johnson captured Niagara and the fight at La Belle Famille. I gave a pipe tomahawk for her, which I borrowed of Levi, the sutler. She was eight and spoke only in the Messessagey tongue and was terrified of my skin and beard.

Since then, I have taken thirty-three back from the savages, some with a sack over their heads and their arms pinned to their bodies with rawhide ropes. They take a powerful lot of saving to bring them back, and even then I am convinced they are always sad.

I remember being called to Sunday dinner at Spraker's Drift by the Noses to see a boy I had returned the year before. He sat across from me at table in a ruffled shirt and swallowtail coat, with a Spenser periwig on top of his head and a chain round his ankle and bolted to the floor.

I could take Alice the same way, but some doubt prevents me. Why am I here? Who is the other? What is he saying?

At the moment, I am without pain.

Captain William Johnson, also known as Tageheunto or William of Canajoharie (he is no captain, only we called him that when he was a boy because of the airs he put on), rode in last night with a dozen warriors, including Captain Sun Fish—the Negro Seneca from Conesus; Twenty Belts; and Hiakatoo, who has forty scalps in his house on the Genesee and is married to a white girl named Jemison.

Tageheunto has been up the Susquehanna watching Clinton's army for a week. He says the Rebels blew the dam at the foot of Lake Otsego three days before. Two hundred bateaux loaded with matériel went rushing downriver, riding a wild wave crest six feet high for thirty miles with the soldiers racing along the banks to keep up. They will link up with Sullivan any day. Then there will be five thousand, with Parr's Rifles and the artillery.

My Messessageys draw back to the edge of the empty village when the Nottaways come in, ever wary and suspicious of their old enemies but especially of Tageheunto, who is half-mad and has been reported dead twice by the Rebel newspapers. Though so far he has gone unwounded, and the credulous say bullets pass through him as if he were smoke. He is one of Sir William Johnson's sons by a squaw in the Mohawk castle. When he was drunk, he used to talk about his horses and hunting dogs and the slaves and the big house he would inherit from his father. But the old baronet died, leaving him nothing but his name.

Tageheunto wears a dashing cocked hat, a red coat with epaulets, and his long black hair tied in a queue. And he can write, which is a rare accomplishment among the savages. But he paints his face black on one side and red on the other and uses a hatchet in preference to any other weapon. At Cherry Valley, he and Hiakatoo raced ahead of the line to slaughter Colonel Alden, then ran from house to house hacking up women and children. Like me, he is between peoples and does not know who he is, but his rage turns outward in sudden violence, while mine explodes inside my head.

1284205

Though there are but forty of us, we set an ambush for Poor's Brigade, which has detached itself from the main army and begun to probe up the Tioga Creek towards the abandoned village where we camp. We have set such traps before, but General Sullivan has a lawyer's cautiousness. He is afraid of the savages. His army marches by inches, with Parr's Rifles and two Oneida warriors sniffing out the trail in the van and militia far out in the woods on the wings. It feels its way like a huge, blind beast.

Should even a single warrior be spotted in the trees ahead, Sullivan halts, extends his lines, and brings up his artillery. This alternately makes the savages laugh with derision, and rage with frustration. On the whole, though, they are frightened by the size of the beast and its ponderous inevitability. This is not like any war they have fought before; this is a message of a wholly different character.

But Poor is impetuous and craves the glory of slaughtering savages. Hiakatoo and three or four others sit at a campfire in the middle of the village and pretend to be surprised when his skirmishers break cover and begin to fire. The savages melt into the forest beyond the houses, and Poor, without waiting for his guns to spray the underbrush with grapeshot, sends in his men with a jaunty wave of his saber.

We let them follow up the trail a hundred yards where it narrows between the trees, then we open fire and feed the split-faced god at the village entrance. My head begins to pound with the thunder of shooting, and my body shakes with ague or fear. I get a man in my sights but fire high and let him live.

I know him.

Hunsacker is his name.

I Am Old Now
(from Oskar's Book about Indians)

I am old now. Seventy-eight in human years (about 546 in dog years). My adventures are behind me. I drop the mask. I speak in my own voice (which here and there I have interpolated in the text).

This morning I read my wife the papers from Toronto and one from England. The young queen and her German consort vacationed this summer at Breadalbane Castle in the Highlands— my wife says Victoria has secret vantage points cut into the castle walls so that she may watch the servants, grooms, and gardeners without herself being seen. How my wife knows this, and why, in any event, Queen Victoria should wish to spy on her servants, I cannot say. Such prurient interest in the lives of others seems decadent and peculiarly modern. I do not like it.

When she (my wife) falls asleep, I repair quietly to my study and the cluttered escritoire where I keep my maps and notes. I write very little now. Rather I put in time going over scribbled messages from the past, putting them in order for some future historian, or, more likely, some future bonfire. The words are like voices from a distant country. The boy, the captive girl, and their redeemer. And further off, the general. At times, the voices are mere whispers. But on occasion, they rise in a passionate crescendo of violence and exultation.

"In art," Witcacy once said, "there is only form and the extremity of utterance." This was later, after the war, when he taught the Indian children in the little schoolhouse next to Joseph Brant's church in New Oswego.

The voices are muffled, agonized, and sweet.

Mary would have called them shadows and said they come to visit from the grave. No one else hears them but me.

Committee Work

The boy scratches himself behind the ear with the nib of his quill and listens to the sounds of the sleeping house. A clock ticks above the mantelpiece. His brothers shift restlessly in the loft on their corncob mattresses. One of the girls pees noisily in a pot in the next room. His mother moans and mutters in her sleep. The words are familiar. "Get them out! Get them out! Save them!" It's an old dream. Oskar's mother is constantly struggling to rescue her children from drowning in the holds of ships lost at sea. Someone in the dream, a dark stranger, always holds her back, pinioning her arms, and she is powerless.

Moonlight comes into the kitchen through the half-moon cut above the door to let out witches and evil spirits. The clock and the witches had sailed across the Atlantic with Oskar's grandparents in 1710 on the ship *Lyon*, a German clock and German witches, all the way from Gross Anspach in the Rhine Palatinate, via an English refugee camp on the London heath where four tattooed Mohawk kings came in a carriage one day and offered them land and asylum (or so the story went).

Margrethe Nellis's nightmares recall the leaky *Lyon*, packed with four hundred homeless German Protestants (with their clocks and witches) subject to hot fevers and bloody fluxes. Old Man Death kept the aged seamstresses busy sewing corpses up in shrouds. Until there was no more canvas except what was needed to sail the ship.

Margrethe hadn't even been born yet. Nevertheless she dreams of this.

The boy writes: "dear Genl. Washington, I went to Deygart's (you remember I said he was Chairman of the Committee of Public safety formerly the Committee of Correspondence) & he sent me to Uncle Weemer Klock, my Mother's brother who runs the Committee for Detecting Conspiracies. Weemer said I was a Pusillanimous Rat son of a Tory Rat & ought to be burned out of my Rat Hole & sent to the Simsbury Mines in Connecticutt where the Rest of the Tory Rodents are.

"He held a Gun on me the Whole time though I did not mind as he holds a Gun on everybody since he was caught with the Militia in the Ravine at Oriskany His idiot Daughter Musalina lifted her Skirts in the Door & showed me her nether Hair wch was highly attractive though the rest of her isn't Much.

"He gave me a Letter for Colonel Harper, Chairman of the Committee of Sequestration now in Springfield guarding Clinton's supply Lines. I took Bessie, our last cart Horse wch Toby Catchpole uses for riding to Tice's Tavern in Johnstown, & Tom Wopat came for the Ride on his Pony Pell-Mell.

"We took Clinton's Wagon Road out of Canajoharie but ran into a militia Posse coming back from hunting down a Party of Savages who had Massacred a Family named Hunsicker. They had killed eight Savages but would not show me the Scalps. A Corporal named Ockels requisitioned my Horse in the name of the Continental Congress & gave me a Chit wch I enclose. I would like the full Amount remitted to me as soon as possible as Bessie was a good Horse despite the hoof Rot wch I believe I was getting under control. I hope he treats her better than your man Gimble. I rode aback of Tom the Rest of the way.

"Tom made me open the Letter so he could memorize the Message in case Tories ambushed us & I was killed. I think this a good Plan which should be adopted by the Rest of our Forces in the Future. It was a surprise to me when we slit the Seal & Found nothing written on the Paper Uncle Weemer gave me. But Tom Wopat said it was a Test to see if I was true to the Congress. He said Weemer never trusted anybody till they were Dead & he could see Maggots & besides my Father is a Tory (I have told you this before—moreover, I have disowned him). Tom said we had to deliver the Letter anyway or risk being taken for Spies, wch we did."

The boy writes, thinks, and listens in the dark.

In the next room, his mother's moans rise to a pitch. The boy listens as Toby Catchpole stirs and ladles her a sip of springwater from a pail beside the bed. Oskar does not blame his mother for being ill. He feels like his own brains would burst sometimes. She is a tangle of confusion, atrocity, and mixed allegiances and cannot abide the great split amongst her people. Something soft and human inside her has withered up and ceded over the effort to make sense. She dreams of historical fears and seeks redemption in the Light.

The faint ticktocking of the clock reminds him of his father, and that last night when Hendrick rose eight times to piss and wind the clock, and then took the thing apart to repair the overwound spring before daybreak. Between windings, he had paced up and down the kitchen floor, his stocking feet making the boards creak (which kept the boy awake—he had thought it was his dad's war wound playing up).

In the morning, Hendrick had saddled his mare Miehlke and had ridden off with two hundred savages and loyal whites.

He had told the boy, "I'll be back in a week."

Ticktock. Wind. Ticktock. Wind. Ticktock. Wind.

Oskar thinks he could write a whole book, and there would be nothing in it but questions.

When Approaching Thunder Taught Me to Sing

When they were not killing and scalping, the Indians made passable company if you were not particular about lice and eating well.

Also, the third day they got lost.

Every little setback Scattering Light would take it out on yours truly. He'd do mean things like shooting a musket off next to my ear, which did not help my headache. Or oncet, when Approaching Thunder was out hunting, he painted my face black with charcoal and bear grease and said he was a-going to burn me.

Approaching Thunder hunted by dreams, but, as he later

told me, his dreams did not travel. In his dreams, he was always spotting animals in familiar settings, which he recognized as his personal winter hunting ground beyond the Ononghiara.

One day, when the Indians carelessly left me untied, I made to escape by running into the nearest underbrush. A wild turkey flew up in my face, and I shouted, "Mam!" before I could get holt of myself. I found a nest at my feet with two turkey eggs, which I collected and brought back to camp where they were all laughing at my expense. Approaching Thunder boiled the eggs, which was the only food we had that day.

Approaching Thunder taught me to gird myself with a leathern string and pull it tight to suppress my hunger pangs, but this did not work. He said they were Messessageys, or People of the River Mouth, and that, until recently, they had been at war with the Nottaways, by which I took him to mean the Iroquois roundabout, for he made a motion in a circle and looked somewhat afrighted when he said the name.

Approaching Thunder could speak enough English to make me understand half of what he said, and he sometimes translated when the others spoke, though I quickly began to study the Indian speech myself. I would forget all else—headaches, starvation, exhaustion—to master a new verb, somehow knowing my life depended on it.

The fifth day Scattering Light made hand signs to ask if I had ever eaten human flesh. I managed to tell him surely, but oncet was an old Indian and the meat was too dry and stringy for my personal taste.

That was the first time I saw him smile.

My Christian name is Mary Hunsacker. My Indian name is the One Who Remembers. I was fourteen years old going on fifteen when the Messessageys massacred my family and took me off into captivity.

I had not yet begun to bleed.

I wisht Scattering Light had not knocked me on the head, for the pain only grew worse and liked to have split my skull at the bad times. It gave me evil dreams as well. Oncet I peeked at myself in the still waters of a forest pool where we stopped for refreshment. I looked like an Indian already with my black hair and the buckskin small clothes and leggings Approaching Thunder had loaned me to cover my privates when my shift give out. (He turned his back for me to change, which greatly surprised me as I had not expected such chaste restraint to number among the savage virtues.)

Scattering Light's death maul—a hardwood club with a curved shaft and a smooth, round knot at the end—had dented the side of my skull, which presently commenced to swelling and turned a horrible yellowish purple. Despite Approaching Thunder's ministrations, the bruising advanced down my forehead, into my eye socket, and down my cheek until my whole face was a mask, which nevertheless seemed strangely familiar to me.

On the sixth day, a strange Indian on horseback barred our path, looking fierce, with a bone nose plug, an eagle-feather rosette binding his hair at the side, and a musket slung from his shoulder. This was Pindigegizig, or Hole in the Sky, a friend of theirs who had come a-hunting for them when they failed to show up at a meeting place called Chuknut. Apparently, he was used to hunting them up like this. Approaching Thunder was notorious for getting lost in the woods.

Hole in the Sky examined my head and said they ought to kill me so they could travel light. A big battle was brewing in the forest ahead, and Approaching Thunder's heroes were needed.

I trembled something pitiful at his words, not to mention the rough handling he was giving my head, and then keeled over in a faint. When I woke up, Approaching Thunder was explaining that his daughter had died of the blistering disease in the spring and how his wife had sent him out for the purpose of bringing back another daughter. She would not sleep with him until he did.

I rallied and made them understand that I was sick to death of total strangers discussing my future as though I were an ailing

dog and also something tired of people treating my skull like a
walnut. I said go ahead and kill me. Anything would be better
than wandering around with a bunch of starving savages jawing
all the time about what warriors they were.

Then I fainted again.

When I awoke this time, I made the sign for a dream, at which
they all perked up. I said I seen a boy dancing in a clearing, wearing
an ugly basswood mask with a crook nose and sneering lips. The
mask was divided down the middle like my face, half-black, half-
red. Inside the mask the boy wore a pair of green-glass spectacles,
which made the world look dark and eerie. In my dream, he was
dancing and singing and shooting arrows at the sun.

After this, Approaching Thunder made yet another steaming poultice for my head, and Hole in the Sky said nothing more
about killing me. Hole in the Sky had a haunch of venison in his
saddlebag, which we ate without cooking. The fact that I had
never tasted anything better made me feel somewhat guilty, as
though I was betraying Mam and Pap and Baby Orvis by acquir-
ing savage tastes.

When I had eaten, Approaching Thunder sat with me and
said, "Little daughter, sing me that song."

And I did.

Humbled, We Are Not Yet Broken

This will be our Thermopylae; we feel it in our bones, though it
is amazingly hot and I am suffering from green-corn gut and have
soiled my trousers twice, which is a great embarrassment for a
man my age.

Unfortunately, the savages have already given our position
to the Rebels by shooting at a deer.

Rafe Clench says, "It makes a man wonder why they have
such a reputation for setting ambushes."

I am with Joseph Brant on the line, though Colonel Butler

wanted me to lie up at Chuknut with the sick. My Messessageys have failed to appear. I sent Pindigegizig to bring them in, but they are utterly lost or on their way home, which is more likely. Wabecamegot and I have three muskets and a Ferguson breech-loader. He is a naked flame of vermilion and bear grease. Clench and Henry Huff, two of Brant's Destructives, flank us. They are rough men but good to have in a fight. They paint their faces like savages and, in an oddly feminine gesture, tie a bit of yellow lace in their hair for identification.

We are ready to fling lead, but Sullivan's army moves ponderously, like the future. It made three miles yesterday, barely getting up off the ground and stretching its legs before dropping down again for the night. We have three hundred savages, two hundred and fifty Rangers, and nine Englishman from the King's 8th Foot, which is all the King could spare to save the Indians from destruction.

Colonel John Butler, my neighbor on the Mohawk, commands, though command is an airy thing in this half world between white and Indian. This morning the warriors took counsel together and altered the line in a way that will afford an opening for a Rebel flanking attack. Captain Brant rode across five times, ordering them back to the barricade, but the savages ignored him. Seeing this, Clench exclaimed how he abhorred the savage habit of disobeying their chiefs, which he said makes them natural democrats. He opined that we would be better off if some of them would go and help the other side.

Colonel Butler lisps and stutters and pulls at his queue when his feelings rise. With the savages, he can barely get a word out. I recall his clapboard house high above the river near Dow Fonda's tavern at Caughnawaga, with the catalpa tree in the dooryard and the ponies he kept that were no bigger than dogs and the two bustards with clipped wings named King George and Sir William Johnson.

Last winter he ordered barracks built across the Niagara River, in Messessagey country, for his Rangers and such refugees as had family. In the spring, they planted gardens and began to keep cattle in the ancient savage cornfields now turned to meadow. It smelled of overmuch fatalism to me, and I refused to go. I will die before I turn my back on the war, even for a season, and cross over to Canada.

Walter, John Butler's son, a lieutenant with the Rangers, dreams of yet another form of escape, or transformation. He will become an Englishman and a hero. He envies Joseph Brant his trip across the ocean, his audience with the King, and his portrait painted at the English court. He flaunts a gold-braided tricorne, which seems out of place in the wilderness. And the Redcoats snub him, as they do all colonials.

At two o'clock in the afternoon by Clench's watch, the men stretch and yawn and suddenly see Rebel scouts at the road bend where the Chemung River loops toward us. We lay in a line behind a chain of logs high up a hogback ridge and across the trail, which the Seneca call the Forbidden Path. A wall of scrub-oak slashings conceals our position.

But the Rebels are all technique, cautious and without impulsiveness. They can see a likely spot for an ambush as well as we can, and, when they do, they halt and wait and send a man up a tree with a spyglass.

Caution means they win.

It makes my head pound to think of it.

I shit my guts out in a hole behind the line every five or ten minutes, and I can see the savages losing heart and drifting back out of the battle one by one. We have already lost a fight we did not want, and who knows if the colonel will be able to gather even half this number of warriors to make another stand.

I think of Alice Kissane and get hard. My anger boils up against the Rebels' dumb caution, their method and efficiency. It is a wholly different kind of intelligence than ours, which depends on secrecy and lightning strokes. The Rebels have also learned from the savages, but it is a different lesson.

They will crush us.

Poor and Clinton take their brigades into the woods on our left. Ogden marches to our right along the riverbank. Hand waits in the center for the wings to close, with Maxwell in reserve. They move with reptilian deliberation. And the purpose of their movement is simply to bring as many as possible of their five thousand muskets to bear against our six hundred. We are fighting a lawyer who knows how to prepare a strong case.

When the artillery opens up with canister and grape, the savages begin the Oonah, their wailing call of retreat. The less experienced think we are surrounded because most of the shot falls and explodes behind us where, in fact, it does no harm. This is difficult to explain even to Wabecamegot, who once or twice makes for the horses in the rear, but I have hold of his ankle.

Joseph Brant and the Seneca chief Old Smoke rush to the flank and suggest that the savages there extend their line to meet Poor and Clinton. This idea appeals to only a few who leave their rugged fortifications and dugouts to find new positions among the trees.

"Oonah, oonah, oonah!"

The cry seems to echo in my head. Surely the Rebels must hear it, yet they do not hurry. Their motto seems to be: Low risk and maximum effect.

Presently, we hear the Rangers on the right engaged with Ogden, trying to push by the hogback to take us from behind. We are an island of calm in a sea of battle, or the eye of a whirlwind that swirls souls upward like dusty scraps. When the savages on the flank give way completely, we retire, still without firing a shot, along the hogback and make a circle round the top with the Rangers, Redcoats, and such Indians as care to stand longer. Wabecamegot and I finally get to shoot at people from New Jersey.

I caress my Ferguson, a rare implement of destruction, and spit fire down the hill.

But Poor and Ogden start to pinch us, and the sick and wounded streaming back down the neck of the hill toward Chuknut come under fire. At the top of the hill, we are also close enough together that the canister shot begins to tell. The five thousand Continentals cautiously close in around us. They are military geniuses of caution. We get tired just shooting at them, though they show themselves as little as possible. Nightfall saves them from having to finish us off. Colonel Butler gives the order to retreat. He gives it five or six times because of that speech impediment. Brant cups his palms and calls the Oonah.

Down the hill a woman sings hauntingly, despairingly: "Kwe', kwe', kwe'!"—which is the death song of a warrior.

The night is alive with savage words and Rebel bullets.

Wabecamegot and I struggle back to Chuknut and help load the wounded into canoes before finding our horses and slipping away alone. Mounting, I vomit over Miehlke's withers and feel the viselike grip of a headache coming on. The fiery nimbus inside my head illuminates the night, and the sounds of war go up like sparks, swirling in the sudden light. I reach for my scolper; Wabecamegot reaches to take my reins and lead me. I cannot bear the brightness of it.

Unfinished, the Book Lies before Me
(from Oskar's Book about Indians)

Unfinished, the book lies before me, a jumble of notes and passages copied from sheets of bark and old papers and from the screed of my memory, which was never much anyway.

At night and at odd times during the day, I still hear Witcacy's peremptory summons, his call to battle. My blood gets up. My fingers begin to twitch and itch.

Are you ready? he shouts.

Are you ready to write?

Are you ready to tell the truth?

Yes.

I write: "In those days, we were all writing. Everyone had a notebook. Those who could not write or read wrote in their heads. Even the savages made little marks and drawings on pieces of birch bark or tanned deer hides and called them books.

"We became of a sudden interested in the future, which we sought to know through divination and prophecy and books. Yet we did not understand the future nor the books. We seemed in the grip of some dark destiny of which our enemy had prior knowledge and agreement, a pattern, index, or anathema of events we could not control or ignore.

"My father said he had headaches which were the very template of our predicament. In time, I myself began to suffer an identical discomfort."

Cannibal Heads and Dr. Ryan's Incomparable Worm

"God save the King!" shouts the boy in his sleep, waking himself up. His head rests upon a sheet of paper, half-covered with writing. A guttered candle stands in a puddle of wax by his hand.

The water saint looms in the bedroom door, huge tears splashing down his cheeks. He says, "Your ma's a-goin'. Call the children. We must pray her over."

She has been failing since Hendrick left, failing as the Light has grown. The only medicine Oskar can remember in the house is Maredant's Antiscorbutic Drops and Dr. Ryan's Incomparable Worm Destroying Sugar Plums, which Oskar refused to take after he learned to read and mistook the label to say "Dr. Ryan's Incomparable Worm." Otherwise, Margrethe depended on castor-oil purges and vinegar applications for all family ills, and fed Ephas boiled fox lung for his asthma.

When she first took to her bed, a doctor named Clapsattle had ridden from Schenectady and diagnosed a nervous problem, for which he gave her drops of tincture of castor and liquid laudanum in a sack posset. But her skin had turned dark and her eyes bright, and presently she began to cough up blood, which nothing could cure, though she kept up the sack posset and laudanum.

When Oskar brings his brothers and sisters to Margrethe's room, they are all half-asleep and cross. Ephas wheezes and stands on one foot because of the cold floorboards. Sophronia's hair tumbles down over her face. Kakaphony has a cold and blows her nose in a rag. Toby Catchpole kneels in his nightshirt by the bed with his palms pressed flat together.

He says, "Lord, this is how it be with our sweet Maggie; she lieth now shut up in her fall in a gross, deformed, bestial state. She is not like an angel; she is a bad, thorny bush from which roses may blossom; she is the gross ore wherein the gold is couched and shut up. She cometh to You presently as toward a bright fire for cleansing and refurbishment."

Oskar kneels at the other side of the bed and takes his mother's hand. Her eyes are on Catchpole. Her head is thrown back and her mouth open. A thin trickle of blood emerges from her lips and drops on the pillow. Her breath comes in shallow gasps as quiet as whispers.

"It hath gone hard with Maggie," continues the saint, his sharp nose bobbing at each word, "but she hath seen the Light and cannot be kept from it. She is a horse who smelleth the stable door. Do not judge her harshly for the errors she hath committed, such as marrying Hendrick and afore that when she were a maid at the great hall, which the forces of liberty hath brought low. A woman is a poor shepherd of her desires and a victim of all that is evil in man."

Margrethe's breath catches. She tosses her head slightly. The blood dripping from her lips begins to flow faster.

Suddenly cold, Oskar lets her hand drop.

* * *

A dismal fire crackles and smokes in the kitchen fireplace. It is so pitiful it actually seems to suck heat out of the room and up the chimney. The boy crouches on the hearth with his coat sleeves yanked down over his fingers.

"dear Gen'l Washington, I beg to inform you Gen'l Sullivan has won at Chuknut & all the Senekee Country to Niagara lies Open. I hope I am the First to tell you. I heard from Tom Wopat who happen'd to be down Country when this ocurrd. I warrant the savages and Tories will think twicet before a-rallying us agin If the French join us, we will be Free At Last. (This happened the same Day my Mother died & my Brothers & Sisters are Black with Sorrow tho' I Try to be a Soldier.)

"I have the Pleasure of informing you Also that the Committee has promoted me to Chief Courier of State Secrets & Dispatches. I have a good Horse called Army now & no one can take him from me on Account of I carry the Congress's Commission. In Add'tion, I have become the Mohawk Correspondent for two Newspapers in Boston and Philly wch has afforded me the Wherewithal to make Sundry changes in my Wardrobe (though that Toby Catchpole is alays a-borrowing my Things). Perhaps you have Noticed my Write-ups."

Oskar spits in his inkhorn and swirls it around, trying to eke out the dregs. He begins a new sheet: "dear Beatrice," he writes, "I took a Message to Gen'l Schuyler in albany yesternight & saw yr Husband Wiederpris in the Anteroom he said I Might write you as I introduced Myself as an old Friend of yrs. This is not absolutely True though I wish it were. You may recall we met that day in the Winter four years ago when the Horses ran away. I mean you no Harm by this my Intentions are Honorable & I wish only to Pledge you my undyeing Love and Affection & if you ever need a Favor I am yr Man. Incidentally I am now very High up in the local Committee. Yr Husband Wiederpris can Confirm this. My Ma died recently she alays liked You."

He blows on his fingers and shakes out a cramp. He is not

so much cold as terrified. He spends half the night up, wandering the lonely house in a panicky vigil. He writes and writes, finding excuses to slip away by day to run up the Johnstown road to visit the Polish dwarf Witcacy in his book-lined slave shack, to borrow fresh quills, paper, and ink. Only the writing gives him a sense of certitude and calm. And it's all lies.

Nightmares assail him as soon as his head touches the pillow, a jumble of images. The immigrant ship *Lyon* founders a half-dozen times a night (he has inherited Margrethe's dreams), or bodiless cannibal heads, screaming with their hair streaming out behind, chase him through the dark forest. Aged crones breathe fire instead of words and cast incomprehensible spells over him, or his face grows cold and turns to wood, a horrible mask he cannot remove.

The screaming heads are Mohawk legendary creatures. Tom Wopat told him about them one night and roared with laughter when he saw Oskar's terror. Tom has filled the boy's head with vampire skeletons, stone giants, and pygmies that prey on humans in the forest. They mingle with family stories, his mother's dreams, and his grandmother Berbel Klock's German tales of child-eating witches, men turned into wolves, and mischievous brownies. At night, the Tories come, too. Sometimes they come in reality, but mostly they come in dreams, and the screaming head is Hendrick, his father.

Only the week before, Oskar had ridden west to Little Falls for the committee on his uncle's bay gelding Army, a high stepper with a jerky gait that was hell on his balls, and watched the militia hang Hare and Newberry, two Loyalist scouts.

The militia had tracked Hare to his own home on the Mohawk and surrounded him before giving the alarm. They gave him a drumhead court-martial and hanged him from his own door frame, though his wife pleaded and tried to carry his ankles till they dragged her away. Sergeant Newberry shouted, "God save the King!" twice before they gagged him. His eyes darted violently, then fixed upon his children, who had come to beg leniency. Then he watched them calmly, till the noose went tight and his eyeballs rolled up.

Now Oskar dreams of brave Newberry and his children and of Henry Hare, whom they hung with a sack over his face. Once in his sleep, he plucked up his courage and yanked the hood off. There was nothing but a yellow, grinning skull with blood dripping from its teeth.

"dear Dad," he writes, "Tom W. says as he can get this to you I didn't ask how. I have to inform you that Ma is Dead. Dominie Frederici buried her from the Stein Araby Lutheran Church as she would not be Buried from the Church you built. He wrote her down in his Book—Was laid to rest Margrethe Nellis, wife of Hendrick Nellis at the river, left behind three sons and four daughters, that are all minors. She had numbered 36 years 8 months in this miserable world.

"We had nout for a Stone & you May rest assured I will Kill you if I see you."

Dr. McCausland Give Me a Silver Plate

We missed the battle, which I did not regret on account of I was out of my mind mostly, or in and out of it, and not up to a melee.

I kept hearing the song and dreaming the boy. The words came with the sound of wind in the trees or distant thunder or birds calling. *Oukaquiqua nipoumin, quiticog manido-o-o.* When I first heard it, I had no more than a hundred words of Messessagey and did not know what it meant. Approaching Thunder had to translate for me. *The gods say that we shall die one day.*

Indian songs are short but never end. They go like prayers, but make you want to dance. I thought this one meant I was a-going to die, which was surely what I felt like, but Approaching Thunder said it was a good song, a strong song, that the song would protect me. *Oukaquiqua nipoumin, quiticog manido-o-o. The gods say . . .*

I was riding a whirlwind and did not remember who I was. My face was a mask of pain hiding I knew not what person inside. *Oukaquiqua nipoumin, quiticog manido-o-o.* I was, for example, surely not the child who had fetched Baby Orvis a smack on the ear with a wooden spoon the morning of my capture and then hid in the root cellar with the last piece of maple sugar till Mam found me. It was as if Scattering Light's death maul had split me off from myself and I was over yonder somewhere receding as we marched west, which in the Indian way of thinking is the Land of the Dead (when we would come to it I was not entirely certain).

Approaching Thunder said it was just as well we missed the fight, since the Tories had lost. The Nottaways, he said, probably would have tortured me to death to help them mourn their dead or out of pure cussedness.

Oukaquiqua nipoumin, quiticog manido-o-o.

On the whole, I found I preferred to be out of my mind, as this afforded me ample time to dream about Mam and Pap and Baby Orvis and sing my little song, not to mention its being a painless state. Already the feeling of having a home and a family was disappearing, though I still entertained the notion that Pap might one day come and fetch me back. (To what?) But these savages were becoming a kind of family—Approaching Thunder especially, who seemed avid to share his dreams with me and tell me humorous stories about an Indian named Nanebojo, who could see and shoot out of his asshole.

I even felt a sudden gush of warmth toward Scattering Light, almost, it seemed, because he had struck me. We had that connection. And I could see that he did what he did on account of feeling insecure on this war party. He wasn't but a boy, and the constant fear of getting killed or maybe captured and tortured made him go violent from time to time.

I tried to say something to him with my hands and the little Messessagey I had learned. But it only made him mad. It was as if, trying to be such a brave man, he feared contamination by my sympathy.

When I was not sick with pain from my head, I would try to imagine homey little pictures of the farm, but these generally involved me and Mam and Aunt Annie working about the place like Negroes. We had, in those days, a wood plow and a tree-branch harrow for preparing the land. And since Pap took the horse, Mam and Aunt Annie had to draw the plow whilst I guided the handles. Then there was hoeing, weeding, fencing, woodcutting, and berry picking, not to mention cooking, churning, preserving, spinning, knitting, and sewing.

I loved baking—pitting cherries in the sunlight against the log wall of the house where Mam had planted rhubarb and morning glories, then rolling out the dough and laying it on the brim of the stone oven to rise, and still later rushing back from the hoeing to roll out the dough again, inhaling the baking odors as I pressed in the cherries. When the cake was done, I had something to show. I would carry it from the oven to the table high up so everyone could see and admire. Though mostly Mam and Aunt Annie admired; Pap and Abiel would just tuck in, which, Mam said, was thanks enough.

I remembered a-setting for Baby Orvis, which was the easiest job for a girl, next to berry picking. Sometimes I could let up on entertaining him and devote a moment to myself, not thinking, just feeling how things were and maybe daydreaming a little about Wubbo Ockels, who was the only man who ever paid any attention to me.

When I did wake up, it would be on just those occasions when something unpleasant befell us. Skirting the battlefield at Chuknut, I was mildly alert when we came upon a party of General Sullivan's men skinning the legs off two dead warriors to make boots.

I was about to call out for rescue when I bethought myself and my present savage appearance and realized it might be prudent not to draw the attention of people who skinned Indians in their spare time. As it was, we caught them by surprise, and they seemed not so much aggressive but embarrassed by our presence. No doubt, in the crowd they marched with, this skinning of Indians would make a good story, a yarn told over brandy and cards on a drumhead. Pap might even find such a tale amusing and think to tell it to Mam and Abiel on his return to Fort Plank.

The thought of Pap not knowing that we were all already dead and captured—which was a kind of death—froze me. It was hard to believe he could go happily about the business of fighting and killing and maybe even skinning a few Indians himself while his family was feeding horseflies.

The Rebel soldiers let us slip into the forest without firing a shot, then returned to their hacking, snipping, and slicing.

I wondered what boots made from a person would look like. I wondered how the soldiers' wives would react to human boots. I wondered if you got inside the skin of an Indian, did you feel Indian? If you wore them long enough, would you begin to think like an Indian? On the whole, it did not seem a respectful way to treat the bodies of strangers, and I felt a twinge of shame that my side was doing it.

Approaching Thunder, who liked to discuss philosophy with me along the trail, said the corpses were Nottaway and not worth worrying about.

Messessageys were the only real people.

What was I then?

Messessagey. Nearly.

He said scalps brought eight pounds New York currency at Niagara, even more from Hair-Buyer Hamilton in Fort Detroit. They didn't pay anything for human boots though. He said this with an air of distaste, as though it bothered him to talk about it.

Dr. McCausland, surgeon for the King's 8th Regiment, give me a silver plate for my skull. This was during the retreat, in the Tory camp at Kanadesaga, which was full of wounded Rangers and

Indians. In addition, most everyone there was down with fluxes, fevers, and agues, and a person had to mind where he stepped.

There were two human legs and a hand in a heap in the corner of the Indian house where the Tories had their hospital. Sundry wounded men lay upon the dirt floor a-moaning and calling for their mams.

Dr. McCausland broke the scab, reopened the skin, and splashed hot red wine on my wound, then smacked his lips and drank off the rest.

He wore a ruffled shirt pulled up to his elbows and knee breeches, silk stockings and buckled shoes, and a butcher's bib apron, much soiled with blood. A little drummer boy, no older'n me, held his coat and saber and a copy of Horace Wiseman's *Surgery*, to which the doctor would refer at every turn, wetting his bloody index finger with his tongue and rifling the pages and humming, "Mmmm, mmmm—" when he came upon a helpful passage.

The boy's eyes kept darting every which way, from the pile of limbs to my head to Approaching Thunder.

Dr. McCausland give me arsenic grains and laudanum in a mug of brandy to dull my senses.

A smith came in with a portable anvil and a ball peen hammer. McCausland tossed the remains of a meal from a silver plate on the table into the corner with the legs and bade the smith pound the plate thin as paper and cut him a piece as large as a sovereign.

Ping, ping, ping went the hammer.

Oukaquiqua nipoumin, quiticog manido-o-o, the song went.

I recall the doctor said, "I ain't ever done this before."

And the drummer boy fainted.

Ping. Ping. Ping.

Black Minqua Sorcerer Defeats Sullivan with Human Sacrifice

My headaches are nothing but confused thoughts coming to consciousness. You cannot know what you don't know, think what has not been thought. What I suffer is the terrible pain of the unknown and unthought pressing against the inside surface of my skull.

The things I see I do not recognize and seem but a whirling chaos, like a myriad dust devils spinning in a hundred colors and shapes. This war has ruptured the pristine surface of our mental existence. Demons and spirits swirl up through the breach. We who hold to the old will be pressed to the wall, and beyond, into the marches. This is my nightmare. Why am I here? I ask myself. Who is the other? What is he saying?

I do not say that I did not covet the savages' land, but likewise I did not wish them off the face of the earth. My model was Sir William Johnson, the baronet, who stripped himself in the forest, bedaubed himself with paint and animal grease, danced the dance, and struck the war post with his tomahawk. There was no measured cynicism, no self-righteous acquisitiveness in this. He loved to dance. He loved to bed with savage females. His many offspring are like the seeds of his ideas. He was more Irish than English in his tolerance; something alive ran through him which he had in common with everything else alive, savage or white. But he is dead, and only a few of us remember.

The five thousand Republicans seething up the trail behind us are the shape of a grand new idea, which I abhor. They destroy everything in their path, scorching the earth, the earth-colored savages, and their villages. They watch the forest itself with suspicion, measuring it with a cold, acquisitive eye. It is this measured, yet total, destructiveness which unnerves me.

They are the future.
I am against the future.

My Messessageys slip in under cover of a storm. By the look in their eyes, I can see their minds are already across the Niagara, and they will not tarry. I try my skill at persuasion, but one might as well try to stop the wind. And it does no good to blame them or to tell them that thither they are walking out of history to a place where there is no redemption, only a black silence. To their way of thinking, they are in the right. Moreover they have captured a wounded white girl but will not sell her for anything. Dr. McCausland of the 8th operated and removed half a cup of dark matter from her brain. He says she will not live.

Tom W. also rejoins, melting into the retreating column one late afternoon astride Pell-Mell as we march past Conesus— sometimes Sullivan's advance scouts find our cook fires still burning, they are so close. He bears news of the committee at Fonda and a letter from my oldest boy who is a Republican and a sorry person more worried about what the neighbors think than the state of his own soul or the debt he owes his father. He never liked the savages and despises me for my association.

In his letter, Oskar says Margrethe has gone west, as the savages put it, which can only mean she is in a better place. I spur Miehlke ahead till I am alone in the forest and think of her, which is a kind of prayer. I mind when she was a girl and would bring her yellow puppy Finch down the lane to show me when I rode by. I would give her a leg up, and she would ride while I walked for half a mile, and we would talk about the dog, a ribbon she had ordered from New York, or the wandering artist who cut her silhouette out of black paper and tried to grasp her hand in the cow barn.

I vow we were happy then.

Surely, we all thought, this dark cloud of war would pass without a shot, and, after the shots came, when the British army made its landing in force. We never dreamt of such a disaster as befell Gentleman Johnny on the fields at Saratoga. And now that disaster seems more like a betrayal as those same British who promised to restore us temporize and withhold their might. It is hard that my wife died a-hating me when I was far away because of ignorant fat men in curled wigs in a city called London. The thought bears me off in a whirlwind of anger, which is still like a prayer or a cry of pain.

I am in a rage again; but the pain follows Margrethe west. I send it to accompany her, my shade with her shade.

At Little Beard's Town on the Genesee River, four hundred of us go forth to meet Sullivan and grimly set our ambush. I lie up with Clench and the Seneca Hiakatoo, whose skin is a map of tattoos and scars. Two of his sons by the white captive Jemison are also with us. One is drunk.

But Sullivan's caution, which we are now used to, ruins our surprise.

A scout of forty men falls into our trap, not the whole five thousand. We kill eighteen, and the rest escape save for an Oneida, a young officer, and a sergeant. The Oneida dies at once, quickly and horribly, with his digits, then limbs, off one by one, and his eyes gouged with a burning stick. He is no one. He has turned against his own brothers.

We question the officer, Boyd, and his sergeant as we retire. Boyd is intelligent and terrified and glad to be among white men whom he trusts to defend him from savages. But at Little Beard's Town the warriors send a deputation under a Black Minqua sorcerer named Crow, one of an ancient tribe from the shores of the Lake of the Eries. His people live together in a village by Buffalo Creek under the protection of the Seneca. Crow's face is painted half-black, half-red, like the Whirlwind, the split-faced god the savages sometimes call the One Who Protects Us. It means he is half-spirit and half-human, half-dead and half-alive, a medium for the magical forces of the forest, a messenger from the Land of the Dead.

He demands the white prisoners from Butler. The savages

will abandon us if they cannot work their rude magic, if they cannot call their protectors in the ancient way. Where are the English soldiers? he asks. Where are the big guns that can mow the Bostons down like grass before the wind?

Butler is sick of dealing with savages, sick of wheedling, bribing, and placating them. I can see this in his face. The savages think nothing of begging a gift of us before they lift a finger to help. They have grown to depend on our gifts, our guns, powder, and iron goods, yet their arrogance passeth understanding. Like us, they have completely misconceived the other. Ours is a dialogue of colliding misapprehensions. Butler turns pale and stutters a weak objection, then mounts his horse and leads his Rangers out of the village.

The savages drink rum, which they call darling water, and strip the white men and tie them to a post. Crow dances and sings to Agreskwe, the sun, the Iroquois god of war. He mimes shooting the sun with an invisible musket and smites unseen enemies, brandishing their scalps in triumph. Water drums and sacred turtle-shell rattles din an eerie rhythm. The savage songs rise into the autumn air.

Somewhere in the distance Sullivan's scouts pick up the airborne sound and wonder.

The hair goes up the back of their necks.

The savages set fires at their victims' feet and peel the skin from their chests with scolpers. They shoot muskets point-blank without loading balls so that the burning powder penetrates the flesh of the bound men and turns them black. The sergeant screams at me for aid or to shoot him, and the savages allow me to minister to him with water. Boyd whispers encouragement. He repeats his prayers. The muscles of his neck stand out like cords in his effort not to cry out. He has dreamed of a white man's glory but found another sort among the savages.

They rip out his fingernails and bite the joints in twain, and his screams go up to the savage god.

The sun shines a white heat.

He watches Crow, a mixture of disgust and hatred and terror in his eyes.

Boyd and the sorcerer are having a conversation, a dialogue of pain, a dual prayer.

Crow paints Boyd's face in a facsimile of his own, then cuts a strip from Boyd's forearm, inserts a stick, and pops out the tendons, which writhe like white worms of pain upon his tattered flesh. The savages call this caressing. And to them it is a form of love, a spell against death. They incorporate the other by sacrificing him to their spirits. They live in a world of dream, as do we all, though it is a different dream from ours.

I watch in a daze of horror as Crow puts glowing coals to Boyd's penis and testicles while warriors bite the flesh from the sergeant's shoulders in a frenzy. Should either victim fall unconscious the savages bring him water and offer him food or brandy as refreshment, waiting until he is conscious enough to resume the ceremony of pain.

At length, Crow seizes Boyd's hair and pulls his head back so that his chest arches toward the sun. The savage priest thrusts a stone knife into the soldier's chest and rips him open with a wrench. Plunging his hand into the cavity, Crow tears Boyd's heart from its moorings. He holds it aloft and shrieks in triumph. A low moan rises from the savages.

The sun receives the heart.

Down the trail, doubt enters the hearts of Sullivan's troopers; a cloud seems to pass over their souls.

It is ancient Iroquois magic, though the Rebels have no way of knowing this. It is the lore of the Forbidden Path, the savages reverting to their former habits. And the gods answer one more time. One last time.

For Sullivan comes no farther than Little Beard's Town.

His soldiers find Boyd's head upon a log, with his tongue cut out and his eyes gone. They find the sergeant with the flesh eaten off his shoulders (by dogs, they say to one another, preferring not to think the truth). They burn the town and girdle the orchards and make a pyre of the green cornfields. And then, mysteriously, they turn away from Niagara. They march east, burning the empty Cayuga towns between the lakes, then south to the Chemung and the safety of the fort they built before Chuknut.

No one knows why they turn back.

No one knows.

The Feast of Dreams
November 1779–February 1780

Death, the Faceless

The boy bears down on his goose quill, splattering dribbles of homemade ink on the curling paper. His tongue protrudes and licks his upper lip in his effort of concentration.

"Are you ready to write?" Witcacy asks. "Are you ready to tell the truth?"

"Yes."

Witcacy stands under four feet tall in his stocking feet, with a humpback that seems to rise higher behind than his outsized head in front. Smallpox scars crater his sallow cheeks. His huge nose, flattened by a horse kick when he was a boy in Lodz, spreads across his face like a cauliflower.

Witcacy frowns. He says, "If you lie like that, you'll never learn to write."

"I amn't lying."

Witcacy hops up on a copy of Burton's *Anatomy of Melancholy*, which sits atop *Tristram Shandy*, which rests upon the satires of Menippus and Lucian, John Dee's *Monas Hieroglyphica*, Fludd's *Utriusque Cosmi Historia*, and an *Arte of Rhetorique*, so he can peer over the boy's shoulder. In the same motion he strikes Oskar across the ear with a stropping belt.

"Truth is beauty. Look around you," he shouts, then trips off his perch, picks himself up, and snatches his violin from the floor with a flourish. "The savages are poetry come to life. Their every gesture is rhetorical. Beauty is truth to them. In order to tell their truth you have to forget the world and render everything poetical."

". . . render poetical," writes Oskar, rubbing his cheek. "I don't understand," he says.

"Plato hated poets," says Witcacy. "It's crucial. We took a wrong turn there. Plato hated Indians. You have to overcome writing."

"But you taught me—"

"White boys have to learn the long way around."

Oskar sighs and tears up his sheet.

Only this isn't happening. He remembers.

He remembers the hunchbacked violinist who played seventeen years of nightly performances at Johnson Hall, told jokes, juggled plates, and farted in key, sleeping all day with his Ibo mistress, Queenie, in a slave shack the bowmeister gave him. Oskar remembers the shack, his first classroom, books running up the walls to the ceiling on rough-cut planks with bark still adhering to their edges and pitch falling like a slow amber rain. The books that didn't fit on shelves spread across the floor like a forest tangle, here and there arranged in steps and platforms for Witcacy's convenience. One wall was honeycombed with pigeonholes, cupboards, and drawers containing the dwarf's collection of Indian bark scrolls and wampum belts, five glass cases of New World butterflies, a dozen bushels of stone points and potsherds, and a stuffed owl. The table where Oskar sat practicing his letters was cluttered with a microscope, a brass orrery, dusty beakers, mortars, pestles, glass tubes and rods, and mysterious jars full of viscous liquids and fine powders—what Witcacy called his philosophical apparatus.

Are you ready to write? Are you ready to tell the truth?

Yes.

Whack.

The black girl snores and mutters on the narrow, short bed next to the cooking fire, a thin quilt spread over her splayed knees, the ritual scars on her ebony cheeks smiling blackly like so many little mouths. From time to time, she stirs, thrusts out a pink-soled foot, and adjusts the iron pot-crane.

The memory of those scars makes Oskar feel queasy. The girl's dusky skin has always seemed masklike and alien. He cannot abide the thought of Witcacy lying with her. Recalled to the present by a pang of doubt, he thinks of his beloved fair-skinned Beatrice married to her Hudson Valley patroon. Catchpole and Sophronia cuddle together in the bed in the next room, making the rope springs creak. Their whispers and laughter fill him with foreboding.

His eye lights on Tom Wopat, who squats in a corner of the Nellis kitchen, rubbing a finished mask with bear fat and offering it shreds of Indian tobacco from a broken cup beside him on the floor. Tom calls this feeding the mask. As he applies the fat, Tom speaks to the mask in a low voice, telling it about the man he is selling it to, telling it what is expected from a good mask in the way of cures and protection. The mask looks suspiciously like a Continental soldier in a miniature cocked hat, pouting his lips and whistling.

"dear Gen'l Washington," the boy writes, "I wish to report a terrible Wrong as has been Commit'd by the Troops under Coll. Gansevoort upon their Return from the recent Campaign against the Senekees. This happen'd on Sept 29 & my Intelligence was Mistaken wch I forwarded to you within the Week.

"The Savages attacked were not Tory Indians but four christian Families loyal to Congress who lived peaceably aside the River not fer from here at Ft. Hunter around the Church. The Indians put up no Resistance (the Troops kill'd Three anyhow) & were sent down to albany to the Gaol there & th'r Houses and Goods taken over by some poor River Folk wch Tom W. calls Pig People on Account of their Poverty and low Way of Life.

"Little Abraham who the Ft. Hunter Mohawks call their

Kinge is now in Gaol & ailing. The River Folk say they will not budge even if the Indians come back as Indians ought not live in better Houses than Whites. (They are former Tenants of my Grandpa Klock who settl'd them on Land he got of a drunken Canajoharie tho the Indians dispute it.)"

Then the boy takes a sheaf of folded papers from his coat pocket (the fire has gone out for lack of tending). Across the top of the first page, he has written: "For the book on Indians."

He quickly begins writing where he left off: "Mohawk is not a Mohawk word but means Cannibals in some other Language. The Mohawks call themselves the Flint People wch shows how Senseless Savages can be as there is no Flint hereabouts. They worship Idols in the Shape of ugly Masks cut from Basswood Trees. They hold several Mis-Apprehensions—the Constellation we call Orion or the Hunter's Belt by them is thought to be the crooked Lips of a Hunchback called He Defends Us. They also believe the Earth is really the Carapace of a very large Snapping Turtle."

The boy looks up from his page and remembers the crooked lips of Witcacy, who has a tic and often twists his mouth toward his ear in a way that resembles Tom Wopat's grisly masks.

Sometimes Oskar falls into a kind of vertigo; the masks and people around him seem to grow to resemble one another. The masks and the world—the dwarf Witcacy, the masks and their secret humpback masters, his mother's face grimacing in death, even the stars in the heavens—converge despite his attempts to keep them apart. Everything is a sign of everything else, and Oskar is lost in a circular whirl of interchangeability based on masks.

The masks, Tom tells him, are called Faces. The Iroquois put faces everywhere. Their clay pipes have tiny etched faces facing the smoker. They carve faces on their hickory war clubs. They carve tiny faces on bits of wood or weave them out of corn husks and carry them as amulets.

Everything has a face.

Another name for Death is Without a Face.

Oskar shakes off the thought, inchoate and chilling. Cold air rushing under the cracked door flaps at his cheeks like bird wings. Lately, Oskar has been dreaming of death.

He writes in a rush: "dear Beatrice, I write again as a Friend tho you have not answer'd my Letters. We are in Evil Times. The Troops returned from the Senekee Campaign with Tales of Savage Enormities the like of wch I have ne'er heard. Two Captives, Lt. Boyd & his Sgt., were horribly Mutilated especially in their Privy Parts wch I should not speak of except that it affears me what might happen to you should you be Captured. (I have meditated on this often & at length.) To be sure, if you were Captured I Should Follow & track you to the Ends of the Earth at any Cost in Pain & Blood. & tho you be Mutilated I would Love thee and Nurse thy wounded Parts.

"I hear from Tom W. that yr Husband Weiderpris intends a visit to the Upper Forts to settle Accounts for Victuals with the Quartermasters who are in Arrears. If you wrote me a Letter you were to accompany him, I would meet you Somewheres. As like as not I Shall be terrible kil't soon in my Endeavors for the Congress and the Press but I would die better in Mind if I had spoke with you oncet. If you could give me some Remembrance like a Hanky, I would a-carry it into Battle & die Happy.

"I am yr Slave Always, Oskar."

Folding his papers, he bundles himself up. He ties rags around his feet and hands and throws the stiff leather dispatch case across his shoulders. Flurries dust the darkening trees and rooftops. The hard earth bangs like iron against his toes through the rags. Army stamps his hooves in the cold stable.

After saddling the horse, Oskar waves good-bye to Tom, who, for once, has other business. He intends to chance the icy drift on Pell-Mell and deliver his masks on the other side of the river. Tom Wopat has started a new line of turtle-shell rattles, which the pagan Mohawk use for dancing and casting spells. He pulls such a rattle from his bag and hefts it above his head by the neck as Oskar mounts. Oskar can just see the beaked mouth gaping against the paler skin of Tom Wopat's wrist. The sound of the rattle startles Army, who skitters out the yard onto the turnpike, nearly throwing the boy before regulating his gait.

Across the valley, autumn lightning flickers, and thunder rumbles distantly. Oskar rides east past the limestone Palatine Church, which the Germans built on land his father donated on the west bank of Caroga Creek. The bronze cock atop the weather vane soars like a black idol in the twilit sky. Toby Catchpole said the cock was meant to remind the parish of the rooster that called St. Peter three times to repentance. Oskar wonders if his father will ever repent, if he could ever redeem himself after all he has done.

Beyond the church, Army canters across the stone bridge over the creek and veers into the yard at Fox's tavern and gristmill, where the Committee of Correspondence held its first meeting in June 1774, a week before Sir William died. Oskar can hear the river crashing against the log landing at the mouth of the creek, just out of sight behind the mill. Along the eastern shore of the creek, a narrow path runs up out of the valley into the rocky hills, past the ruins of an ancient Indian castle Witcacy had discovered, toward Ephratah.

Chairman Deygart, Fox, and Oskar's Uncle Weemer hand over their letters at the door and toss him a parcel of cheese and rock-hard bread. In five minutes, Oskar is on his way again, setting Army at an easy trot in the direction of Albany. Tiny flashes of light seem to follow him in the woods—the moon shining off the river, he thinks. But there is no moon. In an hour he reaches the dark wall of Anthony's Nose, which shoulders down to the river as if trying to push unwary travelers into the rushing water.

Just as he reaches the frozen turnpike's narrowest point, Oskar hears a shout. A shape like a face that is nothing but lines and dots rides out of the trees. Oskar sees light glinting off the lock of a cavalry pistol. Army rears as Oskar yanks on the check-rein. The boy slides off over the gelding's haunches and dives for the cold brush at the side of the road. At the same moment, a naked arm snakes around his throat and heaves him up on his feet. Two men drag him deeper into the undergrowth by the cliff face. They clamber up slabs of rock slick with ice, cracking his shins and dislodging his foot rags.

There is an old cave partway up the Nose. His father told him about it. He has never seen it before. But now he can see a dim glimmer of light deep in the rock. The Indian on his left wears a red coat with epaulets. His face is split down the middle with paint. But the man on his right is huge and black and wears no paint. He seems to have no face at all.

Oskar struggles at the mouth of the cave, but the two men force him in. He drops on his hands and knees, and they kick him twice to make him crawl toward the fire. He looks up at last and spies a lonely figure huddled up to the flame, wrapped in a worn trade blanket, sipping something hot from a blackened ket-tle. With the light of the fire and the shadow of the kettle, the face is like a mask. But Oskar would know his father anywhere.

In the Town the White Bones Lie

On the whole, having my head sawed open and a silver plate put in was no more painful than having red-hot spikes driven through my eyeballs. I immediately got worse and about died. My face blew up like a pumpkin. I dreamt I found myself in a house that resembled the farmhouse at Fort Plank, though it was dusty and dingy and uninhabited. Food was set at the table, but I had the strongest feeling that no one would ever come to eat it. The emp-tiness of the place was so dreary I about lay down on the floor and cried. But outside I heard a person singing that song, the song the masked boy sang as he shot arrows at the sun. *Ouka-quiqua nipoumin, quiticog manido-o-o. Oukaquiqua nipoumin, quiticog manido-o-o.* The singer stumbled over the words as though they were unfamiliar and foreign. But his voice was stern and sweet, and I felt the words pushing me out of the house.

The gods say that we shall die one day.
The gods say that we shall die one day.
The gods say that we shall die one day.
The gods say. . . .

Sometime during the night Approaching Thunder woke us, saying we must join the retreat on account of General Sullivan's men, with Pap and the soldiers in Indian boots, who were close behind like a trail of ants after dead meat. He and the others had to take turns carrying me on their backs like a baby.

We crossed the Niagara River three days later, though I did not see the falls (Kahkajewang) on account of being delirious. I do recall Approaching Thunder making a fuss about getting into the canoe and having to toss tobacco into the river to placate Nzagima, the Great Snake, who lives under the water. The Great Snake—A.T. says he's as big as a house—can swim under land as well, which is a disturbing thought, Nzagima zipping around just beneath your feet like a giant mole getting ready to burst through and swallow any human being who happens to be about. The only thing that protects the Anishinabe, or Real People—as the Messessagey call themselves—is the Thunderers who throw down lightning bolts every time Nzagima threatens to pop up. Sometimes, though, he is on our side. Apparently, he was a big help in the last war with the Nottaways. "Nottaway" means "snakes" in Messessagey. And the Messessagey word for a man's dingle-dangle is "snake head"—"kinebigustigwan."

Approaching Thunder is afraid of all manner of creepy-crawly things. Oncet we had to stop for nigh half an afternoon because a toad jumped on the path before us. Approaching Thunder said it was an evil manido sent by some sorcerer to kill him. He and the other Indians sat on the path, burnt tobacco, and sang songs to the toad till I went up and shooed it away with the hem of my worn-out shift. I do not recall this, but was told about

it later. Later still, it became a legend told at the winter camps—
"How the One Who Remembers Fought the Toad."

Oncet I woke up and asked him why Scattering Light was
afraid of me. Approaching Thunder said the boy was affeared I
would use my woman's medicine to avenge the blow from his
death maul, which he had not meant to give me but only did so
in a moment of thoughtlessness. Approaching Thunder said perhaps an evil manido or a sorcerer had taken possession of Scattering Light's shadow.

The Indians say we are made up of three parts: body, soul,
and shadow. When we die, the body rots, the soul goes west to
the Land of the Dead, where Nanebojo rules, and the shadow
stays around the grave, sometimes bothering ordinary living folk,
whom it somewhat envies. The soul lives in the heart. The shadow
lives in the brain. Soul and shadow can sometimes separate from
the body and wander off on their own, which was what was happening to me.

A.T. said I would be altogether there one minute and the
next my eyes would close and my soul and shadow would be out
traveling all over the map. He was always asking me what I saw
when my eyes were closed, or if I'd learned any new songs. But
mostly he was affeared my soul and shadow might forget to come
back one time, which happens, too.

Approaching Thunder's name in Indian was Pahoombwawinn-
dung, but he generally preferred for me to call him Uncle. He was
about as old as Pap, with skin like leather and a little wispy mustache that he thought was handsome but wasn't. Scattering Light
was Saswayahsega, but I was supposed to call him Cousin. Pleasant Wind was Manoonooding. Bird on the Wing was Cheehock.
They called the Continental soldiers "kitchemokomon," which
means "Big Knives," and Approaching Thunder taught me a song
that went: *Kitchimokomon ododanong / Wawsigineshinon,* or *In the
town, the white bones of the Big Knives lie.*

A.T. said the town was Boston, where the Rebels came from, and the song foretold their defeat at the hands of the Messessagey. The words twined through my head like threads of light, coming back and back as we traveled along the forest tracks. They were a message from somewhere else.

In the town, the white bones lie.

It made me think of Baby Orvis and Mam and Aunt Annie and Grampa Hunsacker a-lying in the fields with their hair off. It blended with another song, the one I'd heard in the dream and sung for Approaching Thunder.

Oukaquiqua nipoumin, quiticog manido-o-o.
The gods say that we shall die one day.

Oncet we were in Canada, Approaching Thunder had no trouble dreaming meat. Deer and wild turkeys seemed to walk onto the path in front of us and wait to be killed. One day a cloud of pigeons flew so low the Indians could knock them down with their musket butts.

Approaching Thunder made a soup for me of pigeon bones and dried corn he dug up at a former campsite, which would have been excellent save for his practice of cleaning his hair and throwing lice into the kettle while he cooked.

I was too weak to eat much, but A.T. soaked a portion of cloth torn from my shift in the broth and made me suck on it like a baby.

We were headed west, as I say. I was vaguely aware of this. And always on our left was a vast expanse of water the color of quicksilver, which the Messessagey called Wahbeshkegookeche-game, which means White Water Lake. Approaching Thunder said it was a bad place to travel by canoe (chemong), being so near Nzagima's home. The Great Snake could slip out of his hole under the falls at any moment and cause such a storm as no human could survive. Nights, we camped on sand beaches with the tiny lake waves lapping gently at our feet and a fire crackling

and throwing up sparks towards the stars, which I had never seen
in such abundance.

Approaching Thunder threw away the dirty bandage Dr.
McCausland had tied round my head, replacing it with one of his
own made with duck down soaked in a decoction of ground dogbane root and applied, still warm, to my wound. He said if I would
stay alive till we reached his castle, he'd find an old wabeno
woman he knew who would cure me with a spell.

I said what was a wabeno woman, and why didn't he just
shoot me.

He said I must sing my song.

I told him the last thing I felt like was singing.

I was certain I would die, which did not bother me much,
as at least I'd be out of the pain. I kept drifting into unconscious-
ness, which I confused with being dead. I dreamt of Mam and
Pap and Wubbo Ockels and what he did with his fingers by Clinton's wagon road to Lake Otsego. Approaching Thunder said I
should take advantage of my dreams to visit the old woman in
the moon. He said this one morning while putting the duck-down
poultice on and getting me ready to travel. I thought he was crazy.
But then I slept again, and in my sleep I heard a voice singing,
and Nokomis came to me. She beckoned, just at the edge of the
fire glow, and I followed her, climbing a ladder to her lodge,
which hung in the night sky, surrounded by stars.

One day I woke up and the pain was gone. The leaves were gone
from the trees as well, and there was a fine dusting of snow upon
the ground. I wasn't anywhere I could recall walking to, so part
of me judged that I was dead. I half expected to see Mam and
Baby Orvis at any moment, or have Romulus bound up from the
water's edge and lick my face off.

I had been a-dreaming of them, though in my dreams there
was something never quite right. They were asleep and I couldn't
wake them. Or the weather would be hellish hot and they couldn't

get warm. Oncet I was building a building, and they all came and watched without saying a word or lending a hand. Romulus allays looked afrighted and confused, as though he was seeing things I couldn't. Later, Approaching Thunder said these were their shadows come to visit, to say good-bye, and that I saw them with my shadow.

The first person I saw after I woke up was the old wabeno woman Wabanooqua, Lady of the Morning, who had been a-caring for me. I was laid out in the open air before a small hut of bulrushes, wrapped in a bearskin and smelling of same. Wabanooqua had a fire going next to her in the sand, with a blackened kettle steaming on a couple of rocks.

She sat with her back to me, singing.

Oukaquiqua nipoumin, quiticog manido-o-o.

The gods say that we shall die one day.

Before I could say anything, she reached into the fire and snatched a live coal out. She threw it in the air a couple of times, catching it and rubbing it between her palms. Then she popped it into her mouth, shut her eyes, and let a faint column of smoke or steam escape her lips. Turning to me, she spat the coal back in her hand and threw it into the fire.

She said, "That's a good song you got. I been practicing with it. I always used to burn myself even with a mouthful of goose grease."

She laughed, and her laughter issued from her mouth like smoke.

She Walks the Sky Guesses My Dream

In the forest, civilizations clash, just as in my head, humors, ideas, and words contend willy-nilly till my skull feels like a bucket of raging demons. It seems impossible that we can come to know what we do not already know. Yet, in my dreams, I begin to comprehend the shape of something unthought. The Americans—this word now becomes part of the new vocabulary in our camps, replacing "Rebels" and "Bostonians"—seem willing to trade truth for freedom, which is their way of winning the argument.

There is a woman, living in a village toward the Ohio, the savages call Ji-gon-sa-seh, the Mother of the World, or the Mother of Nations. She speaks the ancient Attiwandaronk tongue, which is hardly but a memory everywhere else. They say she is a lineal descendant of the first woman on earth and possesses the gift of prophecy. One day I intend to visit her, if the Lord lets me live that long.

The candle casts a black shadow across the boy's face when he enters the cave, so that I can make out but half his expression. The half that I see is terrified, yet filled with hate. It would do no good to tell him that yesternight, and the night before, I sat upon Margrethe's grave, conversing with her in the sleet and dark. Our conversation was like a prayer, and as one-sided. Or that I have dreamt of her every night since news of her death reached me.

(I take her body in my lustful arms and she laughs and suddenly begins to decompose, even as I enter her, a circumstance which both horrifies and excites me. Her eyes become black holes, her breasts wither, her lengthy tresses slip back to reveal the green cups of her cheeks, an odor of putrefaction assails my nostrils. Yet I continue the act of procreation, as though I am somewise bound to her. When I wake, I am hard as an iron spike for Death; the people about me say I have wakened them with my shouts.)

And so I say nothing to the boy, covering my confusion and doubt with hurried preparations for our departure.

The Mohawk call this cave the Navel, and it has some sacred meaning for them. Deeper in, there are obscure drawings upon the walls, which even they cannot interpret. Before we leave, I place my hand on his shoulder and draw the boy with me and, holding the candle high, show him the pictures. He is trembling. I believe he thinks I mean to slaughter him before the pagan images. The fact that he mistrusts me makes me tremble with anger. In my mind, I pick up a rock and beat his brains in. I feel a headache coming on. The images swirl—a message I cannot decode.

Around my neck, on a rawhide thong, I carry a tiny carved face, no bigger than my thumb. It is a Whirlwind mask, painted half-red, half-black. She gave it to me when she guessed my dream, as is the custom among the Iroquois.

It is the face of my dream.

This is how I remember it. She dances a step or two and takes my hand. "I will guess your dream," she says, "and the dream will cure you."

Up and down the river, pagan choirs lift their voices and utter the great hymn of mourning.

Woe! Woe! they sing.

Hearken ye!

We are diminished!

This is during the autumn feast, when the False Face dancers perform the traveling rite, visiting every house to drive off plagues and evil spirits, and anyone who wants to can call for a curing. Only there are no houses or crops, and thousands of savages camp along the Niagara from the tumbledown trenches of La Belle Famille as far as the Upper Landing.

Woe! Woe! they sing.

Hearken ye!

We are diminished!

Woe! Woe!

The cleared land has become a thicket.

Woe! Woe!

The clear places are deserted.

Woe!

The thirteen strings of wampum are worn out in mourning. "I will guess your dream," she says.

*   *   *

Her husband is already dead. He took himself away in the Indian manner, chewing raw muskrat root, which we call water hemlock (*Cicuta maculata*).

Woe! Woe!

Hearken ye!

She says the muskrat root appeared to him in the night, calling him like a woman. Captain Brant's Negro manservant, Antophilus, who brings me the news, says otherwise. He laughs ill-naturedly and says the Mingo drank too much and was afraid of She Walks the Sky. When he got drunk he would grow melancholy and sit with the barrel of a musket in his mouth as though smoking a pipe, or he would weep and threaten to hang himself, saying he could not bear to face his wife.

I think it more likely he did not know what he was afraid of, that his wife only became that thing in his mind because she was white and shared the strangeness of the other he could not name. The savages here have plenty to be afraid of, only it is difficult to explain it to them. (Perhaps the other he feared was only the future and the thing that has no face.)

We are all being swept away by an idea, part of an old argument suddenly made flesh. And, of course, the British insist we cannot tell the savages the truth of our situation lest they throw down their arms or go over to the enemy.

Woe! Woe!

The savages eat the muskrat root raw. Even a small portion is enough to kill. It causes internal bleeding, diarrhea, vomiting, and violent convulsions.

Woe! Woe!

"I will guess your dream," she says, "and the dream will cure you."

The dancers dance. The shaggy False Faces shake their rattles and blow ashes on the mourners. Wabecamegot has crossed over to spend the winter in the hunting camps of the Messessagey. Butler's Rangers have retired to their barracks on the cleared ground opposite Fort Niagara. They have dug gardens and built a cow barn to supplement the army stores, which must be shipped from Montreal at great expense.

The barracks and gardens are in Canada. The sight of them makes me feel we are already giving up, that we have lost the war. I cannot look that way.

The structure of everything is smashed, and the effort it takes to reassemble the parts each day is exhausting (she says I could see it as a dance instead of a chore).

Woe! Woe!

The cleared land has become a thicket.

Woe! Woe!

The clear places are deserted.

Woe!

Up and down the river, the Iroquois nations mourn their dead warriors and ruined villages. They say the roll call of the chiefs' names and recount the beginnings of their confederacy (their civil poetry is their great art), but they have no houses, no crops, nor winter clothing. The very young and old are already weak from fever and simple starvation.

"I will guess your dream," she says, "and the dream will cure you."

In my heart, I believe it is foolery, but I am forced to join the savage rites to humor her.

As it happens, I have dreamed a dream. It comes often, whenever I have a headache. When the pain fades, I fall asleep, or doze, and go into a gray world. I am building a house. I am up on the roof, tacking hand-split shingles. Margrethe and the children stand at the foot of the ladder, watching. No one lends a hand or says a word. My boy Oskar points and draws their attention to some aspect of my work. But I cannot hear his words. When I climb down the ladder, they make way for me without a sound. I look back, and the house is ramshackle and rotten. Suddenly, I am inside the house. It is fiercely hot, like a day in July, yet my father shivers beneath a quilt and says he cannot get warm. His skin is white. He shivers and turns his face to the wall. Then I am hunting with Margrethe's yellow dog Finch down by the river flats. Finch barks at the air, furious at something I cannot see, then runs away. An old Indian named Abraham squats on the cobble beach, shaking a handful of tiny animal bones like dice. From time to time, he throws the bones and shouts, "Ho! Ho!" The clicking of the animal bones sounds like a rattlesnake's warning. When Abraham turns his face to me, it is tattooed and painted in a hideous design, one half red, the other black.

Woe! Woe! the singers sing.

The dancers dance. The shaggy False Faces shake their rattles and blow ashes on the mourners.

The cleared land has become a thicket.

Woe! Woe!

The clear places are deserted.

Woe!

"I will guess your dream," she says, "and the dream will cure you."

Names (from Oskar's Book about Indians)

Of course, the book about Indians is not (a) a book or (b) about Indians. It is about Indians tangentially. And it is incomplete and unorganized, sheaves of notes sewn with a thread, scattered about.

I write: "The important thing to remember is about names. The Iroquois have a set of names which they give out over and over again. They are people ruled by names. When a child is born, the parents go to the Keeper of Names to find out what names are free at the moment. When someone dies, his name goes back into the list of available names. As often as not, his family will find a replacement by adopting a captive taken in war. The captive takes the dead person's name and becomes the person. It is as if the same person has lived for hundreds of years. No one dies, and there is no such thing as history, only legend and myth."

But the truth is I do not understand the savages. I try to say this and this, but they evade me. Difference is their primary characteristic. It envelops them in a luminous sheath. They seem marvelous, more real than real. They become everything that is not familiar, expected, and routine. They become the mystic other, the female, the child, and the self, which I glimpse only fleetingly. I invest them with all my hopes, ideals, and graces. At the same time, I am inordinately disappointed when an Indian begs, steals, acts stupidly, or cruelly, goes about in rags, or drinks too much (I am more than familiar with these human failings).

When I see an Indian—and it is rare that you see one these days; they are fading from the earth—I become jaded with all the old sentences.

Night Traveling and the One-Eyed Man

Oskar's father has kidnapped him because of a dream, and now absence defines the boy's life. Oskar has disappeared into the vast, black nullity of the forest the way Hendrick did years before and thinks of nothing but what he has left behind. He misses the farm and the comforting sight of the church steeple by the creek at the edge of the property. He misses his brothers and sisters. He misses Witcacy and Tom Wopat. Most of all, he misses Beatrice, who seems, after their initial meeting, to be drifting further and further from his phantom embraces. He even misses the water saint, whose beatings gave him something tangible to resist, to hate. Hating Toby Catchpole made Oskar a person.

He suffers nightmares when he sleeps, imagining himself locked in the hold of a ship, the crowded compartment filling with screams and moans as the vessel founders. Sometimes he reaches a hatch and manages to open it despite the ship's rolling and the waves crashing across the decks. But suddenly the ship turns turtle, and he falls through into nothingness. Falling. Falling. The ship's prow is carved with the head of a lion.

He recalls Margrethe's stories of the vineyards of Gross Anspach (which she had never seen), and remembering, he suddenly
begins to understand her feeling for what she had lost, how everything was a sign of loss for her, how that came out in her
yearning for the Light.

Nothing is as Oskar expected it would be.

The night at the Navel they gave him a green Ranger coat
and a uniform cap to wear under his cloak. If he escaped, they
told him, the Rebels would take him for a Tory spy and kill him.
They didn't even tie his hands. Then they rode across the river
at Spraker's Drift and spent the rest of the night with Tory Indians at Canajoharie within sight of Fox's mill and the tiny dock
at the mouth of the Caroga. In the morning, Hendrick pulled a
patch down over his left eye, which made him, suddenly, unrec-
ognizable. And all that first day, he was out in the valley, visiting
Tory sympathizers, collecting supplies and recruits, without a soul
knowing who he really was.

At night, they crossed the river and rode west. At the farm
gate, Hendrick stopped and sat a spell, with his hands resting on
the saddle, and let Miehlke crop frozen spears of grass by the side
of the road. Once or twice she lifted her head and sniffed the
wind and danced nervously as if she remembered the place and
was anxious to be bedded down in the familiar stable.

They went slowly and were never recognized. Days, they
slept before roaring fires while strangers stood watch at their shut-
tered windows with loaded muskets. A dozen times Oskar could
have escaped, but terror prevented him. Tageheunto always rode
at his side, the black Seneca Sun Fish, his cheeks rippled with
initiation scars, a little behind. Far ahead, jog trotting to the next
stopping place, rode a one-eyed man he barely knew, but who
would always find him.

One morning at dawn, Hendrick nudged Oskar awake with the
toe of his boot and stood over him, proffering the boy's own letter
in his dirty clenched fist.

The boy read: "We had nout for a Stone & you May rest assured I will Kill you if I see you."

Oskar could see his father's hand shaking. He could see his father's scleras flashing yellow in the dull glow of the fire. With his free hand, Hendrick held out a heavy dragoon pistol, butt first. Oskar could see the flint hammer was cocked, the gun ready to fire. He took the gun, which he nearly dropped because of the weight of it, and slowly got to his feet, shivering from terror and the morning chill.

"Make a clean shot, Boy," said Hendrick.

Oskar fought to hold the sleet-slippery pistol level with his father's chest, but his wrists grew suddenly weary; sleep tugged at his eyelids. The skin of his father's face was drawn back in a mask. A tiny scab pulsed in the middle of his forehead.

Hendrick said, "I have a paper for you to sign. It transfers the deed for a hundred acres of timber you got when my father died two years ago. It were meant for me. You have an objection?"

Oskar signed.

When they left him alone, he wrote his commander in chief.

"dear Gen'l Washington, I write this in Blood (not my own, but from a Hog the Savages kilt for Supper) on a Bit of Elm Bark & will leave it on the Trail for Someone to find. I have been took by Hendrick, my Father, whom you know Something of. It is not my Fault the Dispatches were took too. I hope it were Nought important but in Case it was you'd better change yr Plans. They have not a-harmed me but I da'est not attempt to Escape at the Present Time because I am watch'd so Closely. The Pig was not so Bloody so I must close. I hope they do not Torture me. tom Wopat will find this & send it on. I hope our Men do not shoot me by Mistake. The Tories are brazen & do not fear Capture Yrs. Oskar Nellis."

And then he wrote to Beatrice.

"dear Beatrice, I rite you a Last Letter in Blood. The Worst has happen'd & I find Myself in a most Melancholy Condition. Before they took me, I gave a Good Account of Myself, you may be sure. But there was upward of a Score of Savages wch surrounded me. Do not grieve for me. I am not worth a Tear from yr Eye. Maybe we will meet in Heaven. I am glad you will not see my Corps after the Savages have done with it. Yrs Eternally, O.N."

A week after Oskar's capture, they no longer had to travel by night. They marched in military order with scouts in front and on their flanks, driving a herd of cattle before them for food, each cow carrying a bag of flour and a bag of salt draped on either side of its neck.

Tom Wopat caught up with them on Pell-Mell, joining what was now a column of thirty men, five women, and eleven children, mostly on foot. He melted into the column from the brush on the side of the trail, his head wrapped in a blanket, the trudging figures mirrored in his green-glass spectacles. In his skinny hand he carried a contraption of wires, canvas, and bamboo, which, unfurled, shielded his head from the sleet and rain. His face was like a mask.

He trotted past Oskar with a nod, rode to the head of the column, and handed a sheaf of elm-bark scrolls picked up from the trail to Oskar's father (messages sent, but received by the wrong person). He said not a word, but disappeared again within an hour.

The first day at Fort Niagara, they raise Oskar to a lieutenant in the Indian Department, his father's corps. They do this without asking him, without ceremony, as soon as he enters the fort. Someone tells him to draw his kit from the quartermaster and where to stable his horse. Someone else offers to buy his teeth. They assign him a party of Shawnee warriors to lead, though he cannot speak Shawnee. The Shawnee are fierce-looking warriors with fur capes and feathers down to their shoulders and a superior air. Maybe twenty of them.

Oskar thinks, Who am I? He wonders how to get back to what he was. If this is possible. Even his attitude to his father has changed. Hendrick was easy to hate in absentia. Now he is the only person Oskar feels any connection with, though Oskar does not know if Hendrick wants to punish him or protect him. This ambiguity makes talking a burden. When he finally turns to ask Hendrick what to do with the savages, he sees only his father's back disappearing into the House of Peace to report to Colonel Bolton.

Oskar sees men he recognizes from the old days in the Mohawk Valley, pitiless men who, like his father, were once heroes in an earlier war, or just plain farmers and traders, men with sudden reputations for violence and rapine, men with prices on their heads. But mostly they are standing around in nondescript homespun clothes and shapeless hats in the freezing mud of the parade ground, looking bored. (Now, Oskar thinks, he also has a price on his head—automatic with the lieutenancy. Would Uncle Weemer ever believe he hadn't stolen Army on purpose and gone over to the enemy? He remembers Henry Hare's wife begging for his life, the slow hanging from the door frame.)

The Shawnee wander off and come back a while later without their fur cloaks, carrying a small keg of trade brandy. They offer Oskar a drink, which he declines.

In the afternoon, the Rangers shoot a deserter named Enos Watts against the wall by the Gate of the Five Nations.

Someone tells Oskar Watts's story. Indians had come upon his place one day and stolen a cow and a pig and a half peck of dried corn at the point of a gun. His next-door neighbor had taken the opportunity to avenge an old feud about a line fence and turned Watts in to the local committee as a Tory sympathizer. The committee had sent up an armed band of milly-men when

Watts was in Johnstown buying harness. They shot his eldest boy running away and arrested his wife, mother-in-law, and three remaining children. The mother-in-law then died a month later of a chill she received marching to the county jail. The militia burned Watts's barn and let the neighbor move a family of slaves into the house. Watts swore the oath of allegiance before the committee and went to justice to get his place back, but over the winter they nearly starved. And in the spring he was pressed by a Loyalist recruiter who said they would burn him out come summer if he didn't go for the King. So Watts walked to Niagara where he went down with ague and dysentery and fought for two years in a feeble condition, mostly along the Ohio, far from home. Finally, Watts had begged off sick, which no one minded, as he tended the Ranger livestock on the Canadian side of the river. But tending the livestock had made him homesick for his farm on the Mohawk. He got drunk one night and took off through the woods on a stolen horse. But the horse broke a leg and threw him crossing a half-frozen swamp, and three Indians had tracked him for a reward.

Up against the wall, Watts is pale and trembles so much his knees seem to be doing a little dance. Tears course down the sides of his purple nose, freezing in his mustache. His Adam's apple bounces against his rag scarf.

"Boys," he says, "I hain't seen my wife and childers in nigh three years. My patch is gone to weeds. Boys, I know ye all feel the same. I'd a come back forenenst the summer. I just a-wanted to see the place oncet."

He is talking when they shoot him. Four men in the duty squad fall down on account of drunkenness when their muskets discharge. Enos Watts's crushed beaver hat goes flying when the balls hit him. It lands next to a cone of frozen shit. When the balls strike, Watts is holding out his hand, pleading for his life, though his tone sounds oddly casual, as though he were having a conversation about the weather. The man who offered Oskar money for his teeth strides over to the corpse with his jack-knife open.

In the evening, a fistfight breaks out in a canteen in Dog Town by the river landing, Butler's Rangers against any soldier in a red uniform coat. The riot spreads up the riverbank like a contagion, entering the fort by the Gate of the Five Nations and spilling onto the parade ground. Only the Indians stand by and refuse to be drawn in.

Oskar calculates it will be Christmas in a week.

Playing with the Dead

Besides juggling red-hot coals, Wabanooqua talked to rocks. At first I was some'at surprised at this, especially as they (some, not all) appeared to talk back to her. She had two friendly rocks she kept near the fire to talk with while she cooked or made up medicines. I tried to talk to a rock I found inside the bulrush hut. Wabanooqua nearly split her sides a-laughing. I had made the mistake of addressing a dead rock.

I said hello to one of Wabanooqua's rocks, then held it up to my ear. Nothing. In disgust, I threw it as far as I could over the lake ice in front of the hut. The next morning it was back by the fire. Wabanooqua said it had walked there. Maybe I dreamed this. As time went by, I talked to an alder bush, a wood tortoise, any number of salmon, and a she-bear, but nary a rock.

The Messessagey call witchcraft "playing with the dead." It comes as natural to some, like Wabanooqua, as baking pies and putting up preserves.

I dreamed one night I saw a lion drowning in a vasty sea. People were crawling out of her stomach and trying to swim away. I dreamed I was leading a great army, though all the time I was anxious because the army wasn't mine, and I knew there were people who wanted it back. I dreamed a grim, one-eyed man bayoneted me between the legs, then held me in his arms while the life drained out of me down there. Often a gaunt-faced soldier appeared standing at a wall with his hand outstretched in supplication only to be swept away by a roaring, whirling wind. I was in some strange state between being born and giving birth. I was lying-in, confined, delivering myself. Since I dreamed of Nokomis, my monthly courses had begun. I became familiar with the sharp, rusty smell of my own blood.

In all ways, I was a new person out there on the frozen beach. Memories of Fort Plank and Mam and Pap had the substance of smoke and old fantasies. They were in another world, the existence of which now seemed in doubt.

Sometimes, I would recall the Indian attack, Baby Orvis tugging at my purple nipple, the itching of the hot wheat chaff, Abiel's snuffling, Philomena's shrieks. At such times, I would panic and think, Save me, save me. But when I was myself again, I could not think what I needed saving from. I thought of the dominie shouting, "My Redeemer liveth!" from the pulpit. What was a redeemer? At this time, words began to confuse me.

Oncet when Scattering Light came to drop off food, he sat by me awhile, saying nothing. When he got up to leave, he gave me a snowy-owl feather. This was important, I learned later, as the snowy owl is one of the Thunderers, the Grandfathers who protect the Messessagey from snakes like Nzagima. I flicked my hair back over my shoulder and peered up at him in a way I had practiced with a hand mirror back at Fort Plank.

I wanted him to kiss me and put his hand down there where Wubbo Ockels had touched me. I was suddenly lonely for his fingers. But Messessageys are shy and restrained in matters of emotion, and I did not know the normal signals a girl should give. I only knew he was falling in love with me.

Another time he brought me seven mink skins to make a hat, and I let him hold my hand. And oncet he brought me a red-napped, floppy-eared puppy, which I wanted to call Romulus, after my dog at Fort Plank, but which Scattering Light said was already named Red Dog. (My Messessagey was now tolerably good—I was dreaming in a mixture of Messessagey, German, and English.)

When I told Wabanooqua about my feelings for Scattering Light, she said she had known it all along. She taught me a new song, one her father had taught her:

Ouka tatacouchin nini mouchen-hen.
I hope to see thee soon, my love.
I hope to see thee soon, my love.

Wabanooqua and Approaching Thunder and Scattering Light were closer to me now than anyone. They formed the fabric of my daily concerns. Wabanooqua gossiped about the others, told me their stories, and other stories (since the snakes and toads were underground for the winter, it was safe to tell stories of the Grandfathers, or manidos).

I lay mostly, wrapped in my bearskin, before the door of the bulrush hut, cuddling Red Dog, sleeping, or watching the flat emptiness of the silvery lake ice stretching out to the horizon. Oncet a flock of bustards lit in a pool of meltwater not a hundred feet from where I watched. In the night the water froze, and, when we awoke, the birds were trapped there, squawking and flapping their wings. Wabanooqua went out with her knife and slaughtered them, leaving a little garden of bustard legs sticking up from the ice till the next storm hid them. Oncet a lynx with a bloody foot walked through our camp in the night. Her paw prints were like morning glory petals on the snow. (Red Dog made nary a fuss, from which I concluded he weren't any good for hunting or guarding. Red Dog was only for love.)

And oncet a whistling wind blew up from across the lake, piling thousands of thin sheets of clear ice against the shoreline where we squatted in the bulrush hut. All through the night and the next day the sound of the ice breaking was like the sound of a thousand teacups smashing.

Behind us a steep bluff rose to a crown of pine trees. To

the west, a long, sandy point, flanked by marshes, stabbed into the lake like the blade of a knife.

From Wabanooqua I learned that we were living at the southern edge of Approaching Thunder's winter hunting ground. Wabanooqua and A.T. being related in some way, he was obliged to keep her. But he was suspicious of her wabeno magic and preferred that she live away from his winter camp. Approaching Thunder claimed she scared the animals away. Wabanooqua laughed softly when she told me this. Her laughter, when it came, made me love her, as did the soft sh-sh of her native speech. I could not imagine anyone being afraid of her.

Every few days Approaching Thunder or Scattering Light or one of the other boys would appear without a word, tramping the snow down with their leather-lace snowshoes, and drop off a haunch of venison or moose or a whole beaver, which was like pigs to the Indians.

In a cave hollowed out of the soft clay at the foot of the bluff, Wabanooqua kept a larder full of wild rice in cedar baskets, dried bear and moose meat, lumps of maple sugar, walnuts and berries, and a raft of plants and bits of bone and feathers and other medicines she used for curing: hyssop, pearly everlasting, shadbush, bluestem, dogbane, spikenard, sage, ground plum, lady fern, mugwort and wormwood, wild ginger, puffball, cowslip, ox-eye, mustard, goldenrod, bittersweet, fireweed, and poison hemlock (which she used to smoke in a pipe), and any number of others I learned to name.

Wabanooqua smelled of sage and soft deerskin. Her face had a thousand wrinkles crisscrossed with blue tattoos—lines and semicircles—a mask, or a map, it looked like, with valleys, mountain ranges, roads, and boundary lines.

She was curing me with her possets, powders, and brews, her songs and spells and magic objects, and her knowledge. She was using her wabeno power to heal my head, but the strange thing was she was also teaching me how to be a wabeno. It was like learning recipes from Mam and Aunt Annie. Soon I could boil a love potion as quick as bake a crab apple and currant pie with Aunt Annie's great-grandmother's star pattern forked into the crust.

Wabanooqua taught me her own songs and stories, stories that were like invocations, songs that made you feel better. She boiled up medicines for me to drink and brought me raggedy birch-bark scrolls with pictures painted in red ink made from bloodroot juice. I could make nary a thing out of these except for an image here and there, a man hunting, a canoe, a bear with a man inside. She said she hardly knew what they meant herself. They were ancient things, written and handed down by her grandfathers. Just holding them would knit my head and stop the pain. She said.

(Strangely, if I said the words I began to believe them. Though I always had it in my head that there was another way of talking. I thought, What would Mam say if I started talking about windigos, pawaganaks, and shaking tents? Sometimes I forgot that Mam was dead. She was a voice inside me, nothing more.)

Every evening, by the firelight, Wabanooqua would heat up a pannikin of whiskey, of which she had a large supply. She called it scoutewabo. She said it helped her fly sometimes. And sometimes the Grandfathers came and joined in. The sparks rising from the fire were manidos, Wabanooqua said. The stars were manidos. She had been up there once or twice herself, but preferred not to talk about what she had seen.

The scoutewabo had its own song. It was always the last song I heard before I went to sleep. It went: *Ouka tatacouchin nini mouchen-hen.*

I hope to see thee soon, my love.

I hope to see thee soon, my love.

When she was young, Wabanooqua (I called her Grandmother) said, she had fallen in love with a boy named Annonk, or Star. But though Star dallied with her in the bushes, he would not marry her. (She said she had been born cross-eyed and not comely at all—something like me—but as she grew older she had cured herself of ugliness.)

Her father had been a great sorcerer. In his anger, he had turned the animals away from the hunters whenever Star was nearby. Star and Star's family began to starve. Star's family hired another sorcerer, a man who had his power from Nzagima, the Great Snake, who had given him a piece of his own skin. Star's sorcerer and Wabanooqua's father had fought a great battle on the shore of the lake, not far from where we sat.

The battle dragged on for days, and Star's mother began to feel, in the agony of starvation, a yearning for human meat. This meant she was turning into a windigo, a kind of cannibal giant, which terrorizes the Messessagey winter camps. Star's mother told Star what she feared and asked him to kill her, which is their custom. But Star refused. One day he came home and found his mother skinning the corpse of one of her own daughters. This time he clubbed her to death and built a pyre for her body, which is the only way to kill a windigo, whose heart is made of ice.

No one ever wanted to marry Wabanooqua after that. All the men were afraid of her father. Later they became afraid of her. This was the curse of being a wabeno, she said, and I began to understand how lonely she was.

Ouka tatacouchin nini mouchen-hen.

I hope to see thee soon, my love.

I hope to see thee soon, my love.

Thinking of Scattering Light, I stroked Red Dog's silky ears and hummed the song to myself. But it wasn't my song. And in my dreams the masked dancer in the forest returned to me.

Love in the Starving Time

Snow falls three feet in a week and does not melt. Flesh freezes to iron. I come upon a herd of deer trapped in a draw, their heads and shoulders gnawed by wolves, the rest of their bodies hidden in the snow. (This later seems as nothing; I find humans in a like condition before the weather breaks.)

A rumor sweeps the colonial troops that the French will come in on the side of the Rebels, forcing the English to abandon us in order to save the plantations in the West Indies, which they deem more valuable. Colonel Mason Bolton, the English commander of the fort, says this is untrue.

His cheeks are red as bricks, but the pouches under his eyes are an unhealthy blue-white. One hand is like a claw, with a battle scar in the palm. The hand starts sometimes, as though it had a life of its own. In an improvised shipyard by the Lower Landing, he supervises construction of a ship to be called the *Ontario*, which he dreams will carry him away across the lake of the same name. His sister waits in Bath, writing him letters in her thin, spidery hand. She has a room prepared for his retirement with a workbench by the window. Clocks and watches are his passion. He dreams of the clock striking in the parlor, the cat stirring by the fire, and coal crashing in the grate, sending a flurry of sparks up the chimney (a life cocooned in such events).

Bolton's officers conduct excursions to the falls with the daughters of Tory refugees or female prisoners redeemed from the Indians. Winter dispenses them from the rigors of war, and they create a miniature court for themselves. Their harness bells tinkle cheerily as they gallop past the savage huts and dugouts. They build snow soldiers, dressing them in rags and feathers, and station them at the gates.

Joseph Brant has bought a farm hard by the Lower Landing and installs his half-white wife, Catherine, and his children. A slave serves their meals on silver plate, and Catherine orders the best lace from the government store. Before the war, the chiefs went around in rags. They gave everything away to their brethren out of custom and to balance their exalted position.

We are all dying of starvation or bored or waiting, consumed by nostalgia (the past), fear of betrayal (the present), and thoughts of revenge (the future). I do not know if we are sane or insane, the world is so topsy-turvy. The war is like a whirlwind, and the structures of our lives (army, Indian, colonist) have been upended. Everything is strange. Our former gestures, habits, customs, and beliefs seem inappropriate and wooden. We are automatons acting and thinking in set ways which no longer fit our circumstances.

In the Indian camps, the speakers call the roll of chiefs and try to knit up the unraveled fabric of their society. In the Ranger barracks, the soldiers pray and speak of spring plantings and wives and lovers far away. We all use words to right the upset furniture of our lives, but the words and lives drift further and further apart. We live by the gesture, yet all our motions are problematical.

Woe! Woe! the singers sing.
Hearken ye!
We are diminished!

I have redeemed the boy from the Republicans and She Walks the Sky from the savages. At great risk, I have brought them back to where they belong, though neither one appears grateful, and my headaches are not better. If anything, they are worse. She Walks the Sky just shrugs and whips her black hair back with her hand. She says I must have kidnapped the wrong boy. Then she says redeeming people is only my way of keeping my world organized, and why would I want it organized anyway.

She is full of trick questions, but she is also shy and not so sure of herself as she sounds. I am as strange to her as she to me, and what we do not understand in the other seems at once forbidding and alive.

We are both attracted by differences.

Her white name is Alice Kissane, and she was born in Penn's Colony, south of the Endless Mountains. When she was twelve, her brother's musket blew up in a turkey shoot, sending a sliver of steel through his eye.

"His face was all brasted. I never thought he'd a-quit screaming. The whole family knelt about the bed and kissed the Bible and prayed out loud for him to die. It seemed to me I'd die young too, broken and in agony," says Alice.

She slept for three days and woke up wanting to be bad.

I picture her—a wild child tanned red by the sun, with scraped knees and a torn frock and merry, troubled eyes. She rode a plow horse to death on a bet, led a bear cub home out of the woods. She went after boys in a way that offended the neighbors round about.

"Only the Indians saw no harm in it. They say my soul wants a brother—preferably one that's alive."

The Indians took her because she was wandering in the woods hunting a horned cow, though her father had warned her to let it go. Twice, after she married the Mingo, she went back to visit her folks just to shock them. The second time she only called them from the gate and then rode off in case they had it in mind to capture her.

She Walks the Sky smokes a white clay pipe, drinks trade brandy from a silver baby's cup, and stands square when she talks to you, like a man. Her hands are thick and powerful like a man's, too. She wears a collection of silver brooches that look like war medals or little masks up and down her dress. She has even been tattooed lightly in the Indian way. A thin blue line drops from the septum of her nose to her chin. On either side a curlicue pattern of dots branches outward from the line.

The way she swings her skirts when she walks, the way she whips her hair, the way her eyes burn at you, the cruel, knowing smile she sometimes wears when you want her to be kind—these are all suggestive of a secret abandonment. They trigger unseemly desires in the white men who know of her past among the savages. I am repelled by my own desires.

(There is no more chaste and loving people than the Iroquois when they are among their own. I warrant they care for their children better than any white family. But when the white and Indian mix, all the rules between the sexes appear to break down. In the no-man's-land between peoples, languages, and customs, there is no custom, only naked desire and misunderstanding. It is a childlike state, full of violent experiment—when I think of this I am reminded of the mask of the Whirlwind. Once they have gone there, few ever return.)

Or, perversely, I love those things which at other times I would find repellent. Or what I think is her abandonment is a sign of an individual life that will not be denied, and that life is like a fresh current I desire to join. For me everything is strange, war makes everything strange, and I have misplaced the current of my own life. (She shrugs and says, "There's a lot of that around.")

None of this reminds me of Margrethe, who was meek and indirect and whose bruised eyes followed me with reproach. (Why did she reproach me? I do not know, except that she longed to be taken care of, dreamed of old, lost Edens and courtly doings at Johnson Hall in which she had no part. These were things the world could not provide her, and, of course, I quickly drew back, gave less, because she was insatiable. Sometimes in the night she would start awake shouting, "Save them! Save them!" after which she would say she had dreamed of her family trapped in a foundering ship. It would do no good to tell her that the ship had not sunk, that her family had arrived safe, that she was proof of this. She only frowned at me as though I did not understand.)

Woe! Woe! they sing.
Hearken ye!
We are diminished!

I have headaches.

The pain begins behind my right eye, radiates across my jaw to my ear, snakes up and fills the vein that stands out on my forehead. When the pain reaches my forehead my face is suddenly split in two. The right side is on fire, and the left is in shadow.

She says the pain is a symptom of a soul sickness. (This is the way the Iroquois talk—they say our dreams are but wishes of the soul. But the dream is also a mask, and they speak of dreams as if they were riddles.)

We make love out in the open, swaddled in bear rugs, because she cannot abide being observed. And she has let our cabin out to all her Seneca relatives. She puts her fingers down there and lets me lick them. She makes nary a sound except for a low clicking in her throat seconds before her crisis.

She takes pleasure in letting me watch her piss, the liquid splashing down from her hairy lips, making a deep hole in the snow, steam rising up from the hole. When she does this I am hard as a rampike again. She throws her head back and smiles a strange, rueful smile. She presses my face to her. (Oh yes, we both want to be bad. We take a childish glee in it. It is a magical act, being at once bad and safe and loved.)

One night she idly reaches out from our nest to peel a strip of bark from a black branch jutting from the snow.

Only it is a man's arm.

When I dig around, I discover the corpses of a Conoy family, two women, an infant, and a hunter with his arm raised as though reaching for I know not what (grasping for his soul as it goes upward like smoke). They have died asleep about the embers of a cold fire. Starved or frozen.

We have fornicated in the circle of their rigid arms. We have loved in a sepulcher of death. Later, I dream that the dead hunter embraces us, that he absorbs us, like shadows in a shadow. I start awake and cry out in horror. And She Walks the Sky must hold me till I sleep again.

Woe! Woe! they sing.

Hearken ye!

We are diminished!

Death silences the singers.

Dreams (from Oskar's Book about Indians)

But now I wish to speak of dreams. Scholars of savage lore err in concluding that the native myths and legends are a primitive form of history. They are nothing like history, which is an hypothesis about past events, cast in terms of cause and effect, based on evidence and stretching further and further back in time.

Myths and legends are bizarre little stories which explain the world as if it had formed just yesterday. They are organized like dreams and, in retelling, become the collective dreams of a people. Writing them down would destroy them. (Or the savages are fading now because they are being written—by writing this book, I erase any number of those creatures which I hold most dear, my subjects. The real challenge, the hardest thing of all, is to write a book about Indians.)

The act of memorizing the myths and legends and repeating them keeps them constantly before the savage mind. The savage attention is riveted by its collective dreams in a way unimaginable to readers and writers. (We of the infinitely scattered consciousness—who has not suffered anxiety for the unread? For that matter, who remembers what he has read?)

Savages dream in order to remember; we write in order to forget. Though not even all savages dream alike. The people my father called the Messessagey dream to seek a vision, to find and communicate with a patron manido. The Iroquois regard it as a matter of health and hygiene that the wishes of the soul expressed in dreams be satisfied. The Messessagey keep their dreams a secret. The Iroquois tell their dreams in riddles so that others may guess their meaning.

By writing history down, we try to extend the explanation of the present deep into the past. But the savage, in his dreams, seeks to extend the present laterally, as it were, across the axis of time.

(Would it be possible for an Indian to dream me out of existence while I erase him with my pen?

Yes.)

Oskar Sees the Moon Rise on the Breast of His Beloved

The boy bears down on his goose-quill pen, splattering drops of black English ink on the smudged muster sheets. His tongue protrudes and licks his upper lip in his effort of concentration.

Are you ready to write? he thinks. Are you ready to tell the truth?

Absolutely not.

He writes along the top margin: "Muster Roll of Lt. Oskar Nellis's Shawnee Scout, January, 17, 1780." And underneath: "*Nota Bene.* The following Names are English Names wch Eye give the Shawnee Savages under my Command. Their own Names being impossible."

Dick Redland—Froze to Death.

Miles Short—Gone, Wherebouts Unknown.

Tom—A Drinker but in Good Condition.

Queenie—Lost an Eye in Fight with Rangers.

Steve—Good Man, Hates White People, not to be
       Trusted with Firearm.

Horst—suff'ring from the French Disease.

Boeter Shotts—a White Man who believes himself to
       be an Indian against all Advice to Contrary,
       very Fierce for our Side.

Arnold—Froze to death.

Edward No. 1—Deserted.

Edward No. 2—Brought in Scalp wch He said he
       would sell me for ten Dollars, Scalp possibly
       from Bear or Miles Short.

The boy sighs. He sucks the nib of his pen, staining his lips black. The truth is the Shawnee went home to the Ohio country after the first day.

He writes on a separate sheet, addressed to John Burch, keeper of Indian stores:

"I hereby respectfully request Delivery of Rations & Supplies for the Twelve active Shawnee Indians remaining in my Company. To Wit, the Follo'ing Items:"

12 Bushels Indian corn 6/	3.12-
11 lbs sugar 1/	.11-
1 full grown Hog 1.10/	1.10-
15 lbs butter 1/	.15-
2 oxhides—for making Snowshoes 16/	1.12-
13 Pair of Coating Trousers 20/	9.00-
Two Dozen Buck handled scalping Knives 2/	2.08-
One tailored uniform Coat of Wool Serge	3.00-
One Officer's Sword & Belt	8.00-

Yrs. Lt. O. Nellis.

He pauses and rubs his eyes. It is past three o'clock in the morning. The fire has burned to embers on the huge hearth at the end of the stone room. The whitewashed stone walls sweat tears of condensation. The walls smell of piss. Fifteen men sleep round about on the floor, the benches, and the refectory table. Five Indians and ten colonials. Farting and snoring. From time to time an Indian will shout in his sleep or moan. The Indians, Oskar knows, dream of capture and torture.

A line of dry, parchmenty scalps hangs upon nails in a nogging beam along the barracks wall. One, belonging to an infant, is the size of a Spanish gold piece, with hardly a hair. Colonel Mason Bolton pays for a scalp, same as for prisoners. But scalps carry more compactly. Neither do they stumble and fall upon the trail. Nor whine. Nor beg for scarce food. Nor turn dangerous when you take your eye off them. For savages, Oskar recalls, a scalp is as good as a live person in repairing the loss of a dead relative. Sometimes they even adopt the scalp.

Oskar writes with the concentration of a man already growing shortsighted, his face bent close to the page. A two-inch stub of a candle flickers in a pewter candle holder next to his inkwell. A plate of pork rind and congealed grease, a few boiled peas, and bread crusts sits by his elbow on the long, rough refectory table.

His eyes are red rimmed and fiery. He hasn't slept but in catnaps for a week. When Oskar sleeps, the *Lyon* founders, Enos Watts petitions him for mercy (or he becomes Enos Watts against the wall, watching the lead balls come like angry bees), a lonely girl sits by a vasty lake with a bear for a companion, and a tall, bearded man with one eye relentlessly pursues him. Everything is pregnant with portent and doom. Two nights ago Tom Wopat appeared, dressed in a suit of feathers, wearing a mask and dancing in a forest glade that looked to Oskar like a church. When the dance was done, Tom Wopat said, "Why do you seek to pluck the mystery from my heart?"

He writes: "dear Gen'l Washington, I send you this Secret Letter by a trusted Man who holds no Brief for Tories. We are in grave Danger attempting this Communique. As I may Die at any Moment I will tell you the Truth so that it might be Known (you will have yr Man write Beatrice Weiderpris in the Event?).

"I have sought the Trust of these Tories & have so far convinced them to give me a Commission amongst ye Indians wh're I am able to glean useful Information & Intelligence for the Congress. I will give as quickly as Possible a Summarie of Conditions here—

"Gen'l Sullivan's Attack has left the Savages in sorry Circumstances. They live in Huts & Cavements & suffer Extremely from Fluxes, Poxes & Disorders occasioned by Starvation as well as the Cold and Depth of Snow. I was with my Father yest'day a-throwing Quick Lime into their Burrows where the Dead are by the old Trenches at Labele Famille (this means the beautiful family in the French Language, I don't know why they call it so). The Savages are a great Drain on the Government Purse wch is good for us. Drunkenness and Licence are the Rule. The Savages, the Rangers, the English Soldiers & the Colonials are at each other's Throats. No one lifts a Hand unless the Government agrees to forfeit a Payment.

"I think the Tories & Savages have no more Stomach for Fighting & predict their Collapse by Spring esp. if the Winter goes on so Fierce (I have been to the Falls—they are a Wall of steaming Ice, verie striking to the Eye a Sight I recommend to you if you are ever in this Area My Business Partner says they are a good Spot for an Inn one Day & we are actively seeking Investors Should you be interested in such a Venture we would name the Inn after you).

"Yrs. Oskar Nellis, Spy.

"P.S. I regret to inform you Yr Servant Enos Watts was a-shot a Week & a Fortnight ago when he attempted to escape. I am making Notes toward a Book of Historie about the Campaign to go with my Book on the Indians."

He is the writer of the words, the maker of truth and lies. He takes a bit of broken mirror from his pocket and holds it before his face, seeing the blackened lips (he remembers when he was very small drinking Witcacy's thick homemade ink to ease his hunger). Wondering who he is, who he looks like.

Oskar dips the pen in the ink pot and plants a dot like a scar in the center of his forehead, then drops a line down the middle of his face, dividing left from right. Then he pulls a make-shift leather eye patch over his eye. This is how he feels, split and half-blind, caught between his mother's high-strung and extravagant melancholy and his father's stern and truculent principles (why do they seem always to be acting on a stage with Oskar as their audience?), between Tory and Rebel, between King George and General George, Catchpole and Witcacy, between English and German, between colonist and Indian.

He cannot be who he is, exists only in the line, the trail of ink. Out of the line crawls the worm of words, the writing that both is Oskar and hides Oskar. Are you ready to write? he thinks. Are you ready to tell the truth? The savages tell stories to bring their world into existence. Oskar does the same.

He writes: "dear Beatrice, I take this Opportunity to send you a Message though I will certainly be Dead when you receive it. Any Reports of my Capture by Indians you have heard is False & you need not be Anxious on this Account. I allowed them to believe they had taken me by Surprise & have since won their Trust & Approbation & been given Command of a large Troop of Horse. But my Position is insecure & I may be found out or betrayed at any Moment.

"I have forwarded considerable Intelligence to Gen'l Washington. The Man I send this by is a Friend & Master Dentist (It is of economical interest to note that with so many dead Indians, the Price of Teeth has gone low hereabouts). He has shown me how to sell off my surplus Supplies to Merchants by the Backdoor so as to augment my Salary. This is common Practice & I expect to realize a goodly Sum in the Venture.

"I met my Father's Whore. She is a half-Savage white Woman called Alice (though she will not use this Name). It is a bestial Relation & fills me with Revulsion. She fed me Dog boiled with Corn wch made me ill (I gambolled with the Dog on my Arrival, then she a-slaughtered it before my Eyes!). I saw a dead Indian Woman with her Skirts up over her head & was Hard for Thee. Pardon if I Speak thus but I grow coarse & desperate in this Camp Life. I regret my best Years are wasted in this Place.

"I miss Thee & envy Weiderpris his Free Access to yr Privy Parts. I think you would find me Forward & Adept in that Department nowadays. I think on Thee constantly, esp. yr white

Breasts and Arse, esp. when I see Horses (remembering how we first met). I wish one day you could write me.

"With Love that endures beyond the Grave, Oskar."

When he is finished writing, Oskar folds his letters and drips candle wax along the loose joins. He pockets the letters and slips through the door onto the drill ground. There is a full moon rising. The walls of the fort, the magazines, barracks, and House of Peace are clearly visible.

Stealing through a postern gate into the cleared, snow-covered ground beyond the walls, he thinks, actually, that he likes Alice Kissane. She has a quiet, merry manner and a lewd tongue. No one has ever spoken so boldly to him.

His secret thoughts are sexual. Sometimes Oskar thinks, ashamedly, that these are his only true thoughts. When he thinks of Alice and Beatrice, he gets hard. Strange, forbidden, and forbidding women, more real than real. Their language and their manners are foreign to him, and he can fill the mystery of their gestures with his own meaning.

By the postern gate, he unbuttons himself and begins to masturbate (as he has seen grown men do in the barracks). The moon rises. There is a snowy hill in the distance that reminds Oskar of a breast. (He remembers the dead Indian woman, her black nether hair, the fold of skin, her legging bands cutting into the frozen skin of her thighs.) The moon shines out over the frozen lake. He imagines an Indian girl coming upon him like this, his hand working his cold, engorged, and purple cock. She raises her blanket and shows herself, her tiny black nipples, her hairless nether lips.

She is the spirit of the land. When he is alone in the forest, she comes to him. The moon rises over the breast of the land. Together, he thinks, they will give birth to a new country where everything will be allowed him. The girl turns and bends over, offering him her slim, brown buttocks. (The more sad and des-

perate he becomes, the more he escapes into this secret country.)
He comes with a sigh. Despite the cold, Oskar is sweating.

The Man Who Would Not Look
up at the Stars

The Messessagey went to school in dreams. In sleep, they went
out of themselves. They didn't rest; they changed, traveled, and
held high congress with manidos. They found their power in
dreams. Wabanooqua taught me this.

Out there on the beach, I was getting an education in
dreaming. The masked boy who appeared in my dreams was a
pawaganak, a manido or person who spoke to the Indians in their
sleep. Hunters dreamed mysterious animal tracks which, when
they were awake, led them to the game they needed to feed their
families.

There was a place, also somewhere in the west, where all the
animal tracks converged. No living hunter had ever followed the
dream tracks that far, but I imagined it as some kind of Indian
heaven, a place where all the game congregated.

Oncet I dreamed I lifted my shift in front of a boy (not
Wubbo Ockels or Scattering Light). In my dream, I turned my
back and bent over, trembling with terror and a strange, greedy
joy, feeling that I was submitting without knowing what I was
submitting to. I woke up weeping, with my hand wet between my
legs.

Wabanooqua said I was lucky to have such dreams, since,
in real life, I wasn't much to look at (unlike herself, she said) and
probably wouldn't attract many admirers.

Mornings, Red Dog woke me licking my face. Mornings, I
hummed my song.

Oukaquiqua nipoumin, quiticog manido-o-o.
The gods say that we shall die one day.

The gods say that we shall die one day.

Oncet I remarked how odd it was I had learned a Messessagey song from a Mohawk dancer. Wabanooqua said the mask was my manido, not the dancer. Or the dancer was the mask. (Manidos could change their shapes, grow legs and heads, or disappear—it was sometimes fun to imagine how this could be.) She fondled my head where the silver plate lay beneath the skin and said I had a mask in there just the way she had a miniature bear (I could feel the lump) hidden beneath her shoulder blade. (She had a bear-shaped birthmark on her belly and a rare bear-paw medicine bag that only the greatest conjurers were allowed to carry.) She said Scattering Light's death maul had made a mask of my face. Like her, I would have power but never love. Like her, I would be one of the people and not one of the people. I would be sought out for powders and decoctions yet despised and feared.

Evenings, Wabanooqua drank scoutewabo and sang her song.

Ouka tatacouchin nini mouchen-hen.
I hope to see thee soon, my love.
I hope to see thee soon, my love.

She said all men were weak.

She said dream lovers were the best.

Oncet I thought she said Approaching Thunder's name with a sigh (it allays seemed to me she held him in some particular regard). I knew, though she was old, she was in love. I knew there was something long-standing and disappointing between Wabanooqua and Approaching Thunder.

This is how I knew.

I was in love myself.

One day Scattering Light and Pleasant Wind came trudging down the steep bank to the beach leading Approaching Thunder on a rawhide rope attached to his wrist. A.T.'s deerskins were tattered and soaked, his hair was covered with ashes, and his face had been painted black the way the Messessageys a-painted captives they were about to slaughter.

Scattering Light said they had been up north hunting along the Horn River (Ashkunesheebe) when A.T. had a dream and went crazy on them. Scattering Light said they thought he might be turning into a windigo but wanted to check with the wabeno woman to make sure before killing him. (It was Scattering Light's one character fault that he tended to solve problems by hitting them over the head in preference to any other method.)

Wabanooqua gave him a vexed frown and smacked her lips. She walked up to Approaching Thunder, putting her face next to his face, and said, "What's the matter, old man? What is the trouble you dream of?"

"He won't talk," said Scattering Light. "He had a dream in which the Anishinabe lost their tongues and couldn't speak. So he stopped talking. There was one of those things which the white people make marks in and read. He could read it. It was about the Anishinabe, but the Anishinabe were no more.

"Now he won't speak and he's afraid to go outside. One time he went outside to piss in the night and nearly froze to death clinging to a tree till dawn. He said when he looked up at the stars, he was afraid he would fall off the world."

No one had gone out a-hunting in a week because A.T. said all the animals had fled (neither Scattering Light nor Wabeca-megot nor Hole in the Sky nor any of the others had gone to check on this). Scattering Light said the people were starving (they looked fair fat enough to me) and that it seemed like several others besides A.T. were nigh to turning into windigos.

Now, I never knew a people so worried about their health or peace of mind as the Messessageys. Approaching Thunder was allays complaining of his head or his bladder or an old wound where a bear had scraped him across the buttocks (he was allays a-asking me to examine this). A bad dream could trouble him for a month, so that he muttered about it to himself along the trail and on the hunt (it was allays good to think about something else when you were a-hunting anyway, or so the Messessagey thought).

Whenever he came around, A.T. would sit with Wabanoo-qua discussing his ailments, what might have caused them and what treatment he ought to try. A Messessagey never just plain got sick. There had to be a reason. He'd either done something wrong, insulted a manido, or was the victim of an evil magician hired by his wife or the hunter in the next patch of woods or somebody he'd beat in a shooting match.

Wabanooqua was expert at teasing out a confession, which allays seemed to make Approaching Thunder feel better. She would give him a birch-bark envelope full of powder and send him along, saying, "The bad is behind you. It cannot track you down."

This time, when Approaching Thunder saw me in the door-way, trying to make eyes at Scattering Light while he untangled his feet from his snowshoes, his blackened face went smoky with pallor and the paint began to run from sweat. He said, "Little Daughter, why do you hate me? Why have you put your men-strual blood in my rice pail?"

Then he plopped down on the beach, looking fatigued and confused, and started to sing the warrior's song.

Gago mawimeshikan
Ekwawiyane niboyana
Do not weep,
Woman, at our deaths.
Do not weep,
Woman, at our deaths.

Scattering Light and I took Red Dog and walked up the beach after that, while Wabanooqua sat with Approaching Thunder in the snow.

(She built a little fire to warm his legs and held his hand, not saying much. After, she said to me, "What was there to tell him? He saw the truth. Not about you, but the other, the dream." Nowadays, I know what she meant.)

We found a hollow in the cliff face, which sheltered us from the wind, and built a fire of driftwood logs and threw sticks out on the ice for Red Dog.

Scattering Light said I shouldn't worry, but I could tell *he* was worried. He said he didn't know what the dream meant, but A.T. allays got like this at the hungry time just before winter broke and the sap began to run and bears emerged from their dens. He was allays a-worried he would lose the ability to dream or that the animals would abandon him just when his family needed food the most. So he sometimes dreamed his family was nothing but a pack of fretting, snapping mouths getting ready to eat him up. One year he thought his wife was turning into a windigo and tried to strangle her.

To cheer me up, Scattering Light fetched a carved Messessagey flute from his sack. He played a snatch of some tune or other and sang me a song:

Makatawanikwapun Kwawisiwawitikamakwipun.
I wish to marry a black-haired girl.
I wish to marry a black-haired girl.

But I paid hardly any attention. And Red Dog thought the flute was a stick. Aside from being near murdered by Scattering Light (now forgiven), this was the worst thing that had happened to me among the Messessagey. A.T. was like Pap to me, only kinder, for he never raised a hand against me (while Pap used to recreate in the evenings with a jar of cider in one hand, a hickory switch in the other, and me and Abiel bent over the pig trough with our bare bottoms in the air).

I said, "Tell me that dream again."

And he did—the Indians without tongues, the book about the Indians, Approaching Thunder's sudden ability to read (even I could but spell out a word or two).

I hadn't spent those weeks a-studying dreams with the wabeno witch for nothing. I had a black feeling. It made me scared to be in the world. It made me overflow with sudden tenderness for Scattering Light (still a-singing).

Makatawanikwapun Kwawisiwawitikamakwipun.
I wish to marry a black-haired girl.

I wish to marry a black-haired girl.

All at once I understood what Wabanooqua had been saying, that I would never marry him, that we would never be together, that all life and happiness were brief as a gust of wind. I was losing my family again. I was losing my heart.

I slapped Red Dog away and took Scattering Light's hand and put it down there. I lay down beside the fire. The red sun was high. I let Scattering Light have me in the snow. The cold was nothing. All the time I was saying good-bye.

Turning the Brain
Upside Down
October 1780

A Falling Stone

$\mathcal{T}$he boy bears down on a goose quill, lopped off three inches from the nib for easy packing, splattering dribbles of ink on the printed roster sheets he uses for paper. His tongue protrudes and licks his upper lip in his effort of concentration. Are you ready to tell the truth? he thinks. Are you ready yet?

He writes: "I intend to tell the Truth but It is werrie difficult to grapple with. The Truth is a Mask & its Signe is Division. It is Nought but what lies between Things. It whirls. Yet I believe that to know It is a kind of Madness and a joyful Relief.

"This is what my Father Hendrick said.

"They call my Father Dutch Henry or the Scourge of Schoharie for his Deeds. He is Quick & Hot. You can see it on Men's Faces when he rides along the Column of March or issues an Order. Some say he has the Pox or the French Disease from consorting with Savages. His Eyes are inflamed & run for wch Dr. McCausland prescribes an Ointment wch I believe he bought of the Indians (they say the Dr sewed a silver Plate up in a Girl's Head but she died among the Messessagey).

"Father said he is a falling Stone. He said the Heart is Bipartite when cut open like a Mask. He said for a White Man to become an Indian is like entering a swarming Madness. Becoming an Indian is difficult as knowing the Truth or becoming a Child agin. But it might redeem you.

"Tom Wopat returned my Lettres to Washington and Beatrice. He said he kilt the Dentist. He a-carries a bag of Masks, a Bag of Faces. Tom Wopat's Specialty is ye Storm or Whirlwind Mask wch Pattern he says is werrie olde & its Meaning forgotten. It is the Face of He Defends Us, ye Dweller at the World's Rim, the ancient Father of Masks.

"I write this only for Myself, without Address, having lost my Pre-Texts & Pre-Tences. I am the empty Man, thin as a Line of Ink. I am nought, without Hopes or Memories. I am the Words as they slide off the Nib of my Pen.

"This is all confused but meant to be the black Heart's Truth tho' I meander in't. I'll destroy it when I finish."

Oskar is a falling stone.

He suffers from a quartan fever and shingles. His hair is falling out. When a fever fit comes, he sits awhile beside the trail like a minor earthquake, throwing off a shower of hairs like cornsilk strands. He never sleeps. He has become a stumbling wraith of sleeplessness, addicted to the rush of terror he feels going into battle. Otherwise he peers about and observes his own flashing decline.

He finishes his sentence with a flourish and signs himself with an X and a figured mask (half-white, half-crosshatched). Then he balls up the blank roster sheet and tosses it on the fire. He drains the last of his wake-me-up, a mixture of chicory, ground acorn, and tea laced with maple sugar, already stone cold, and dips his cup in the trickle of springwater running beside him.

In the shadows cast by the tree-log fire, the faces of the sleepers look like masks. A sentinel twenty feet away, hidden among the trees, cocks and recocks his musket, snapping the trigger, to stay awake.

Click. Click. Snap.
Click. Click. Snap.

They have been on the trail eight days out of Oswego and seen nary a soul (besides four escaped slaves eating a rabbit by Wood Creek). Nothing but burned-up villages and farms.

Oskar watches the blackening edges of the paper curl and shrivel and turn to ash. Throwing off the buffalo robe he sleeps under, he unbuttons his trouser front and pisses on the fire. The embers hiss. Smoke and ash float delicately upward.

The night is absolutely black. The air is like a cold, wet linen sheet pressed up against his skin. The minute pieces of black ash are letters that, when they fall to the earth again, will form a message. A coded message no one will read.

Tom Wopat helped.

They scraped Oskar's scalp with a straight razor, leaving a circular lock at the back that hangs down like a horse's tail. They dyed the remaining hair black and braided in shell beads, bits of broken clay-pipe stems, and porcupine quills. (His hair rustles and clicks when he moves. He likes to toss his hair the way a horse tosses its mane.) They stained Oskar's face, scalp, and hands with walnut juice. Now, when Tom Wopat paints him with vermilion and black, his face becomes a mask. It is a terrible sign. No one will recognize him (Oskar thinks) as long as he doesn't take a bath or go swimming.

Oskar even traded clothes with an Indian. He practices walking like an Indian and finds that the world looks different. A chill runs through him, so strong it makes his teeth chatter, whether from dread or fever he cannot tell. What does he dread? *But it might redeem you.*

This is a world turned upside down.

He is riding a whirlwind. His mind thinks: Mask and whirlwind and upside down.

*   *   *

Dawn: Oskar crouches with Tom Wopat by an ancient elm, girdled three feet from the ground and already dying. He holds his hat over his priming pan to keep the powder dry and feels the rain washing away his war paint.

The only way to lead Indians, he has found, is to run faster, shoot better, be more ruthless and braver than they are. Otherwise, they just wander off on their own or join another captain. Since Oskar can't shoot worth a shit and waddles when he runs, he has to take insane chances to keep the respect of his men. Taking insane chances has nearly driven him insane with terror. Not to mention the scars and concussions.

To keep his grit in a fight, Oskar makes up a story about his death. (He is the writer, teller of truth and lies.) He grinds his teeth and thinks of Beatrice. He imagines her coming upon his corpse, pale as marble and naked, stretched over a rock in a mortuary pose. His own death arouses in him feelings of sexual abandon and romance (her hysterical tears, the sight of his genitalia, flaccid but free and exposed for her greedy inspection).

With his eyes shut, Oskar dives through a narrow end window, glazed with newspapers, yellow from age. He cracks his forehead on a bedpost, rolls and flops on the packed earth floor, tangled in a patchwork quilt. He hears the door hinges shriek as the Seneca half-breed named Cornplanter slams through. Somewhere near his face a musket flashes, then roars. He feels a searing pain, a ripple of fire, slink along his shoulder blade. He bounds up from the floor, butting the musket barrel with his head, so hard the weapon goes clattering against the hearthstones.

There is a woman standing before him in a nightdress.

Oh, It Is Bitter, but It Is My Life

That March (what would have been March if I'd still been keeping time the white way), the Messessagey broke their winter hunting camps, and the men, women, and children congregated at their maple-sugar camps. Even Wabanooqua and I were allowed to join in.

Approaching Thunder killed a sow bear and her two cubs along the way, which was a considerable windfall of meat and improved his spirits somewhat. But he was still mostly a sighing gloom.

At the sugaring camp, I met my mother by adoption, Waboonasay, A.T.'s wife. A.T. had given her a scalp to adopt as well on account of having to leave me behind with Wabanooqua, but she said this weren't no substitute. She seemed considerably upset with Approaching Thunder, though in the Messessagey way she made no direct complaints (she pretended to be a terrible cook instead; A.T. was allays a-bringing us a burned duck or a samp with corn kernels parched as hard as bullets). Mostly she said nothing. Especially when Wabanooqua was around.

I said, "Show me that scalp."

When she brought it out, I felt something clutch in my belly, for I recognized Grampa Hunsacker's thin, white locks (his hair had curled over his ears in a way the Fort Plank widows found scarily handsome).

Grampa Hunsacker had been the son of a vintner's assistant in Gross Anspach when a prevalent fever took off his mother, and King Louis sent his armies in to persecute Protestants. The French soldiers raped the women, crushed babies in the grape presses, decapitated the vintner, broke open the wine tuns with hammers, and drank out of their helmets till they puked or fell over unconscious, then collected all the splintered wood to start a fire and threw Grampa's baby sister, Gretchen, on the flames for entertainment.

Afore the Indians kilt him, Grandpa's mind had blanked all this out (even the long trip to England in his father's wheelbarrow). He was the greatest nuisance on account of this, weeping when he didn't get the best bits of food and doing nary a thing to help with farm work—said he was a-watching for grape-stealing Gypsies or playing dolls with Hanale Dochstader in the rose arbor (since we had no arbor, this particularly irritated Mam)—the last instant of his life, he no doubt mistook the Messessagey for Catholics.

Now, to the Indian way of thinking, Grampa Hunsacker was my brother, though still not much for making conversation or helping with the chores. He and I were citizens of another country (his fourth).

During the sap boiling, Scattering Light and I spent every night together, wrapped in a bearskin in a little lean-to he a-built away from the Messessagey camp. We went to bed in our regular places, then sneaked out to be together. He had a sort of earnest, block-headed kindness that made me grateful to him and pity him at the same time. He said I was beautiful (not a majority opinion). He said his snake head wanted to bite me and laughed. I said, "Bite me. Bite me."

Scattering Light said this was the happiest time of the year for the Messessagey, but something in the air belied this, a slight frenzy in the tempo of life, a pushing toward a climax. Wabanoo-qua said it was right for me to notice this. She said the men were already polishing their weapons, that after the salmon fishing came the summer, which was mostly an off-season for the men, a time of war and other sporting events. Approaching Thunder, Wabe-camegot, Pindigegizig, and the others planned to head south across the Niagara to hunt Americans. When they spoke of this, they called the white folk "cattle" and made all manner of disparaging remarks. But I could see the worry in their faces, as if the grammar of their resolve and the structure of the world they were about to meet in battle were different, and they knew it.

From time to time, they told stories of a white man they called the Redeemer (for his habit of seeking white captives amongst the Indians and buying them back—it did not occur to me that I was any longer a candidate for this transaction). The Redeemer was crazy sometimes. Sometimes he would moan and shout and nearly fall from his horse. He would slice his forehead open with a scolper, letting the blood flow down his face and stain his clothes. At such times, the Messessagey believed he was possessed by a manido. His moans and shouts were the moans and shouts of the manido speaking through him.

Like Wabanooqua, like me (perhaps), he spoke with our Grandfathers; he went back and forth between worlds. He was cursed and powerful. And so he was a kind of charm or talisman. Wabecamegot had stood with the Redeemer at Chuknut where he had seemed impervious to the buzzing bullets of the Rebel host. (Wabecamegot also said he had shit a lot, which made the Messessagey roar with laughter.)

Scattering Light, when he painted himself, now began a line of vermilion down the center of his face in imitation of the Redeemer. Then he painted one side of his face red, one side black, and tied a horsetail of porcupine quills to his scalp lock (oncet he stuck me when we were a-making love).

The beads hanging from his hair and ears and the fringe of his leggings went clisp-clisp as he walked. I got to love that sound, especially when he turned at night, and the sound was so faint it was like an emptiness that sucked up every other sound. I loved the smell of him, and the way his scalp lock tossed, so proud and vain and beautiful. I never knew a man with Scattering Light's style.

But I cried and cried when I saw him painted, though I never told him why. I just tried to distract him from the paint with my body (fat chance) and then would lie there a-holding him, fighting against sleep. For in sleep I might dream the dream and see the dancer's mask, with the green-glass eyes glinting out at the world, the arrows going up to the sun.

And it would be the same face, the face of my lover.

The Dream and the Truth

I have headaches.

The pain begins behind my right eye, radiates across my jaw

to my ear, snakes up and fills the vein that stands out on my forehead. When the pain reaches my forehead my face is suddenly split in two.

The right side is on fire, and the left is in shadow.

What I believe is that I am split (we are all split) between what we dream (Indian) and what we fear is true (white).

Four guns saluted us when we marched out. When I bade She Walks the Sky farewell, she whipped her long hair back and shrugged, which infuriated me—only when I am on her does she seem to love me; otherwise, I believe she forgets me as soon as I am out of sight. (Maybe this, too, is untrue.)

Still, this is better than Margrethe, who would whine and wring her hands whenever I went off on a scout and accuse me every time of going across the river to sleep with squaws—her imagination stretched no more than five miles in any direction from the farmhouse. She Walks the Sky makes me want to strangle her, but at least neither of us is apologizing every instant for being alive.

(I believe now that war is a constant, that all is flux, that existence is defined by opposite polarities, which lead to yet other polarities—each signified by a mark or mask—which gives the world a splintering or lightning-bolt pattern. We cleave to words all the more passionately because they are in a constant state of drifting away from us, vanishing as we grasp them. We feel that somehow through the violence of our feelings we will hold them, but we are only left with the sour, ashy taste of old violent feelings and words that no longer mean. In my dreams I sometimes am the woman, am the savage, am the child, am the black man stabbing dolls with pins and killing chickens before a polished wood idol shaped like a tree or a penis. It is all the same.)

We hit Harpersfield at sap-boiling time, catching a party of American militia tapping trees far from the fort. We killed three and took thirteen prisoners, including Colonel Harper. The boy got sick and wailed that he had kilt a man. Then it turned out he hadn't fired his piece. Till then he had stood the marching tolerably well and had stopped writing letters.

An old man among the prisoners could not keep up. The savages painted his face black, led him into the woods, and came back dancing and dandling his scalp upon a ramrod. Joseph Brant kept Harper alive and made him write a letter home telling what gentlemen the Indians were.

I have lost count of the expeditions and depredations since, though I remember standing with Brant fifty yards from the walls of Fort Stanwix in April, with a handful of flaming straw, the sparks scorching my eyebrows, and the Rebels hurling down buckshot and spit. I remember joining a party of Royal Greens in May, when they came marching down from Crown Point along the Sacandaga, and scouting the road ahead through Caughnawaga and Stein Araby (turning north before we crossed the Caroga and reached my former home—I dared not shoot those lonely miles in case I hit someone I was close to). I recall harrying German Flatts and Fort Plank, south of the Mohawk, in August. This time I crossed the river and set fire to my father's house. Later I heard his old Negro slave, Claudius, was up a tree and shinned down the minute we were gone and doused the flames from a rain barrel.

I have put out the word not to fire the church with the bronze cock atop the spire. Why do I do this? Do I hope one day to return and wish to preserve all as I remember it in better times? Do I wish to save the things I labored o'er?

I no longer know where the boy is. He is swept along in the millrace of history. I believe he has learned to love the war though it frightens him. The war nourishes him. I see him from time to time (we all travel the same network of trails and rivers) dressed and painted like an Indian, in a crowd of boys his age. Cornplanter, the half-breed, and his brother, Handsome Lake (thin chested, drunken, and mystical), Tom Wopat (with his bag of faces), and others I cannot remember. They are intoxicated with destruction and irresponsibility. The war nourishes them.

One day I saw a woman crawling in a wheel rut with the

top of her head off and her dress burnt. I went down from my horse, offering her water from my bottle. She died in the road cursing.

It did me some good to hear her.

I am like unto a falling stone in this. The world flashes by. Smoke streams after me like banners in the sky.

I regret nothing. I control nothing. It is a strange delirium. My actions are empty of meaning. I once fought for the King and redeemed lost souls (those who wandered in the wilderness). Now I do the same, but without any reason.

It seems certain that the war is lost, though no one says as much. A French army has landed at Newport. The English stay bottled up in New York for no reason other than temerity and incompetence.

It is astonishing to note the alteration in our attitudes toward the English: I have grown to despise them except for one or two like Mason Bolton. But others, as their fear of abandonment enlarges, become fiercely attached to the King. They are afraid of the new and unknown. They think that by good behavior and proper fealty they can influence the Redcoat generals to save them. It never enters their minds that they have already been forgotten, that the light of the royal eye has passed on, that the will of old England has already been broken by self-doubt and a new idea, that they cannot be saved, their farms redeemed, their families restored.

John Butler's son Walter coughs his lungs out on the march and trembles with ague but wears a lace cravat and makes his horse dance daintily when an army officer is near and writes letters to men of influence. He wishes to be a knight, something old and noble and dead. Others set themselves up in trade at Niagara and make their fortunes selling supplies to the army and the Indian Department (on the principle that a dollar made from the government is the easiest dollar gained). Others still are only tired and weak and stare wistfully across the river, begging the King to give them land in Canada.

This I disdain. I am myself alone.

On the Difficulty of Writing Books (from Oskar's Book about Indians)

Part of the difficulty of writing a book (first impossible project) about Indians (second impossible project) is that the Indians themselves do not recognize our distinction between knowing and being. What they know or say or remember about themselves they are. And they have always been this way (the list of names goes on).

To us, this seems like a comfortable self-delusion. It leads to amazing contradictions. For example, the Iroquois will say that it is important to repeat the exact words of a ritual incantation, song, or myth, otherwise the magic is no good. But it is easy to point out that different speakers tell the stories differently, that the stories, rites, and songs deform (subtly or grossly) over time. The Indians say this doesn't matter. Blithely, they can be reactionary and revolutionary in the same sentence. Though they constantly fret that the old ways (words) are being forgotten, and they are.

Perhaps the truth is that while the words change, the importance of the act of saying them does not. The Indians believe that by telling the stories they are. They exist in the telling of stories, the singing of songs, the dancing of dances.

The book about Indians is against the being of Indians.

I am an old man now. The wife and I call the place where we live the Hermitage. It is made of stone—cool in the summer, warm in winter—and reminds me of Sir William Johnson's great hall in miniature. It is like living in a cave. From the front door you can see the astonishing blue of Lake Ontario down a little avenue of arching elms. Ivy chokes the windows and eaves.

I like the smell of lilacs around the outhouse, lilacs and shit. I must carry the wife there when she goes, she is so infirm. She is drying up and fading away at the same time. The features of her face are becoming indistinct. She feels like a bundle of sticks.

I have a gelding named Army for riding and driving.

There have been five or six horses named Army. I like the name.

From time to time an Indian will show up at the back door and ask politely for a dipper of water. He will say he knew my father. I always cut him a slice of ham and bread, or a piece of berry pie, which I bake myself with the star pattern cut in the crust the way my first wife taught me. Though she wasn't really my wife.

The Indians are a scruffy, run-down lot these days. But the instant we sit in the wicker outdoor chairs by the woodshed door and begin to talk, it is just like old times. Some people run them off like wild dogs. My wife would if she could. She has no time for Indians or the past and finds it difficult to imagine me as a warrior in the forest. In her eyes, I could never have been a hero.

Her eyes brighten when I pull a chair up next to her bed and read the news from England. She knows more about Queen Victoria and Prince Albert than she does about my own past.

I believe she is a good woman nonetheless.

Writing this down, I am destroying my memories and youth. Remembering, I see it all in flashing colors, shouts, and explosions of light. My father said, "We seek in love and war only a moment of true feeling." At the time, I did not understand. I only wanted to kill him. Now I think, Yes. Yes. Yes.

Oskar Beds a Widder

They rage, half-starved, into the outskirts of Ephratah, high up on the Caroga Creek, north of Stein Araby, at dawn. (The Indians don't like to attack this early, especially as the weather is foul, but Oskar has read in a book that Indians attack at dawn. He has convinced them.)

The first three farmsteads they pass are already burned to little piles of ash, with corner posts and doorjambs sticking up like black peg teeth and fieldstone chimneys standing like fat grave markers. Burdock and purslane, wild mustard and vetch choke the cow sheds and privies. A horse-drawn rake, a tree-fork harrow, and a rusting crosscut saw lie scattered about with other bits of machinery like bones about a fox den. (The same rake, harrow, and saw at every burned-out place, it seems. In the whirlwind of war, repetition determines existence.)

The ashes mix with the falling rain, making a greasy paste that clings to Oskar's feet and hands. A black rain falling. Ghosts everywhere (Oskar likes ghosts, people you can't touch or be touched by, people who can't hurt you).

The fourth farmhouse is still standing, a plume of smoke swirling downward from the roof in coils. Two goats strain against their tethers in the dooryard. A half-dozen red chickens forage in the beaten-down grass. There is a privy, a barn, a wagon barn, and two slave shacks in back, all fenced around with cedar rails. Everything smells of wet sawdust and cow shit.

Inside they find a woman setting the plank table for breakfast, porridge bubbling in a black iron kettle on the hob, a teapot steeping on the hot hearthstones, strips of bacon sizzling in a skillet. The woman is wearing naught but a cotton nightdress, a knitted sleeping cap with ear flaps tied under her chin, and a pair of wooden clogs on her stocking feet. She drops a fork with a yelp when the Indians come through the door.

She starts to wail, a long keening cry. She runs two steps one way, then the other. Then she stops and sneezes and looks embarrassed.

"They ain't nobody," she says, whispering to herself it seems. "Cato and Dolly run off. They must've heard them Indians a-comin'. Or they run off a week ago. I lost track. They ain't but me."

She stands there muttering, brushing her scraggly, graying hair with her fingers.

"Yer kin do what yer like," she says. "My husband was took up to Simsbury Mines for a Tory and hain't come back. They ain't no one to protect me. Why I hain't been burned out long ago I dasen't guess."

Without paying any attention to the woman, Oskar's Indians settle themselves on the long split-log benches on either side of the table, and Tom Wopat passes out the porridge and bacon. Cornplanter pours the tea into chipped china cups he finds in a corner cabinet (a family heirloom from the old country, Oskar guesses, wondering which old country).

The woman looks despairing when Cornplanter goes for the cups, but then relaxes when she sees he knows how to use them.

"Thasit, thasit," she whispers. "Make yerselfs to home. There's plenty o' pig in the smokehouse. I like to entertain but my help's a-gone. Yer kin do what yer like. My husband's dead up at Simsbury prison in Connectuckit."

Her chest heaves in great gulping sighs.

Ah-haaa.

Ah-haaa.

Her hands work nervously through her hair, up and down.

Oskar offers her a cup of tea, but she hardly notices him, her eyes flicking from one gaudily painted face to the other.

"This un's courtly fer an Indio," she says. "This un's not a-going ter kill us. Yer kin do what yer like w' me, yer know."

She gives Oskar a sly look.

He cannot guess her age, thirty to fifty she might be, with

her wizened, sun-dried, nut-brown skin and that hank of graying hair. Her breasts swing against the cloth of her shift.

The Indians eat with their knives and fingers, but many whites do the same. They watch Cornplanter drink out of a china cup and follow his example. Over tea, they make general conversation about the war and hunting.

The ordinariness of the scene shocks Oskar. He is so shocked he forgets to eat. Eating and sleeping are ordinary things he has forgotten how to do. His world is all upside down, and Indians sitting politely down to sup on a white woman's breakfast is only a symptom of things generally awry.

The woman beckons him and slips toward the door. Outside, she whispers, "Yer kin do what yer like. I'm a widder. Eat everythin'. Glut yerselfs. I don't mind bein' kilt. My husband's already dead forenenst the winter, over t' Simsbury, took for a Tory. Even I don't know if he were a Tory or not."

She leads Oskar by the hand toward the slave shacks and pushes through the raggedy trade-blanket door.

"Everybody else bin burned out. Yer kin do what yer like. I b'lieve yer torture people afore ye kill 'em. I don't mind. Yer kin tie me to that bedpost there. Whatever ye like. I'm a widder. Yer kin cut up me shift to slavers with yer scolper. Yer kin do what yer like."

She gazes up at Oskar shyly, with her eyelids half-shut, a fierce blush showing through the brownness of her skin.

Ah-haaa.

Ah-haaa, goes her breath.

For Oskar, things suddenly become clear. He reaches and starts to pull her shift up over her head. Above her knees, the skin suddenly goes white and soft and youthful. Only her face and hands and feet are prematurely aged. Everywhere else she is a girl. (Oskar thinks, Was Mama like this beneath her dresses?)

"Anythin' yer like," the woman whispers, making no attempt to help nor hinder him.

Her nether hair is black and coily between her heavy thighs.

Her breasts tug at her chest and sag lushly, their pale nipples angling toward Oskar like a pair of eyes. A web of blue veins makes a map of her chest.

Oskar stops breathing. He believes he'll never breathe again. The woman sighs and leans against him, lowering her arms around his neck. Her breath goes in and out against his neck.

"Yer kin do what yer like," she says.

Head-Piercer, or the Dream of Death

Scattering Light dies. My lover dies. I tell you this so that Oskar will not mislead you.

I never doubted that he would die. I never hoped.

He dies. He dies.

In the early summer, when Scattering Light went to war, Wabanooqua bade me plant a tree. She a-planted one for Approaching Thunder, though she never said the name. The idea was that I could tell how Scattering Light was a-doing on the trail by the state of health of my tree. As long as the tree lived, my lover was alive.

I dug up and replanted a tulip tree I found sprouting in the woods. I buried two half-rotten salmon where its roots would grow and put a little fence around to keep out the rabbits and deer.

Mam always said I weren't any good with plants. Every houseplant she had and a sizable chunk of the vegetable garden I killed by looking at it.

"What if the tree just up and dies?" I asked Wabanooqua. "What if it dies for some reason unconnected with anything that happens to Scattering Light? Say, I forget to water it or the bugs get it?"

She wouldn't answer.

Through the hot days of the summer, I had brought that tree water in an elm-bark bucket and a-sat there talking to the

tree and remembering. Talking to it as if the tree were Scattering
Light.

It was as if I was married to that tree; we were a nation of women
married to trees.

Nights, I was lonely and dreamed my dreams alone, sleeping
with one hand tucked between my legs and the other buried in
Red Dog's neck fur.

Often I was disconsolate for fear my tree was a-dying (though
there was barely a sign yet, only a feeling I had at the sight of a
tiny patch of withering, a brown scale on a leaf—a spot of Scattering Light's blood?—the gray bony remnant of twig that had
already snapped when I planted the seedling).

I had picked a tulip tree (the brilliant, green shoot of Scattering Light's life) because it is the tallest and most noble of trees,
towering above the forest tops. Only a tree like that was fit to
stand in for my dashing lover.

But Wabanooqua shook her head sadly, knowingly. It wasn't
the Messessagey way to exalt oneself. The Grandfathers always
punished a boastful Indian, a magician who became too powerful,
a man who desired too many women, a hunter too successful at
the hunt. A Messessagey was happy in the middle, anxious when
his luck ran too badly (this meant someone was practicing sorcery
against him) or too well. One day my tree would be a stately
monster, a chief among trees, and this would be an invitation for
disaster.

My head hurt less of the time, but when it did hurt I would
fall down in a dead faint, a-seeing colors, whimpering. It felt like
an ax in my forehead (oncet I actually reached up to pull it out),
like my skull had been clove in two. When the pain came in my
sleep, I would dream a man was trying to empty my brains out—
which Wabanooqua said was a dream of death.

In the Land of the Dead, all the animal tracks of this world
converge at a single point, going in and going out. In the Land

of the Dead, the hunters always make a kill and no one starves and no one dies and the prey leaps back into life when the hunter has eaten and dives into the thicket. But the road there is long and difficult. And the Messessagey say a terrible Head-Piercer lies in wait along the way to remove the brains of the dead so that their shadows may remain on earth while their souls continue west.

(Some of the Messessagey had already forgotten how I got my wound—they said instead that I had made the journey to the Land of the Dead and come back, which is why my skin had turned so light.)

The gods say . . .

(He dies, he dies!)

All the while I was studying wabeno magic. And after Scattering Light's death even more so—I became a scholar of the wabeno. Besides possets and potions, I learned how to set a broken bone, how to inject berry juice decoctions and charcoal under the skin with bone needles (this was good against dizzy headaches and joint pain), how to give enemas with a deer's bladder, how to lance boils and infections. An Albany trader had even taught Wabanooqua a way to prevent smallpox by taking a piece of scab from an infected person, letting it dry, and inserting it into a small cut.

In return, I taught Wabanooqua all the remedies and sayings I could remember from Mam, who boiled snakeroot to break a fever or made us drink rhubarb bitters for the runs and swore up and down that sweet potato poultices would save your life from a chest cold.

Mam had other darker secrets. She believed that witches made themselves invisible by holding a certain bone from a black cat between their teeth (the cat had to be stolen and the flesh boiled from its bones at midnight). She said a person would die if a white spider crawled toward him and that the dark spots on a smartweed leaf were drops of the blood of Christ.

Who was Christ? Wabanooqua asked. When I explained, she nodded her head and said he was something like Nanebojo, the one the Messessagey called the Great Rabbit (after this, I dreamed of a huge white rabbit nailed upon a cross, dripping tears of blood upon the grass).

Wabanooqua's world was a battleground between the forces of the air—the great Birds—and the forces of the earth—the Snakes—with the poor Messessagey caught in the middle between darkness and light, truth and lies. She talked this way: Hunger is a man and attacks the Messessagey by making them hungry. Each kind of animal has a leader or chief, and he is a person. The sun and moon and the four directions of the compass are persons. Even the heroes of their stories, our Grandfathers, are people who come to listen when the tellers tell stories on a winter night (or the stories themselves are people—I was never clear on this). The Windigo is a manido in the shape of a giant with a heart of ice. But an ordinary man or woman can turn into a windigo, though you can't tell by looking, only they act crazy and grow fond of human flesh. Witches can swallow a snake and turn into a bear walker, a human being in the shape of a bear. Wabanooqua had seen one once, a dark shape in the woods, spouting fire from its mouth every few steps. She had never brought herself to try the trick.

You could never tell what a thing really was. The world was full of shapeshifters and talking rocks and words that had souls. I myself was both what I was and something more on account of that silver plate in my head, my dream, and my song. But my gifts availed me little because I could not use them for myself— later I would sigh and curse them, as sometimes Wabanooqua did.

The Dream and the Truth

Where am I going? Where have I come from? These questions haunt me in the forest when I am not ill with headache. (Dr.

McCausland has taught me how to bleed myself by severing veins in my legs, but this does no good, though my boots are often full of blood, and the wounds become infected, and I fall fainting on the trail; when I visit Niagara, he prescribes irrigations with acid for my member and gives me drafts of laudanum; they say he operated on a white girl who had gone over to the Indians last year, replacing part of her skull with a silver plate, from which she must have surely died ere now.)

Wabecamegot wakes me standing in an alder grove next to a little pool of water when the action is done. I am not wounded, nor have I fired my rifle. The sun is a drop of blood on the horizon. I have no idea how I came to that place. There is a dead fox next to the pool, its body much eaten by ants and larger predators. Its grisly face smiles up at me like a mask.

A sentinel at the Lower Fort gives the alarum and his company opens fire, though we are at some distance and the balls have no effect. We scorch everything for three miles around and right up to the fort's walls in half a day. We can hear the women inside a-weeping at their losses, which are mostly feed and cattle and some useless horses.

This is how it is now: After four years of war, the Americans have learned how to fight us. Every farmhouse left standing is a fort. The farmers go to ground in their fortified places and try to hold up our advance while their militia assembles on the run to catch us from behind. They sleep in their forts betimes and only emerge to do their chores and haul firewood.

They are quick and careful.

Their messages get through.

They are no longer in terror of the savages (they remain prudent, but not panic-stricken).

They believe their cause is just (it is strange to think my former friends perceive me as a traitor).

Every raid they get closer, kill more, harass us till we lose them in the labyrinth of the forest.

Oskar and his savages are marauding along the lower Scho-harie beyond the Middle Fort. They and others are skirmishers and scouts, preceding our line of march.

I saw him once as we skirted Fort Stanwix, leaving the garrison there to watch the sullen forest, an island in a wilderness sea. He was thinner, burned almost black from the sun and scabby from fly bites. But his muscles were taut as bow strings. And he was dressed like a savage, with his hair cropped and braided in a scalp lock. He swaggered insolently like a savage, too, three scalps slapping at his thigh. It made me angry to see—this insolence, which is only naïveté and false bravado (the savages are doomed, as are we all). When I came close, I saw that his eyes were yellow with ague, that he shook constantly, and that he had been much bruised and wounded about the head.

When we spoke, he would not look me in the face. He said he had passed my farm one day, running from the militia. The barn was burned and all the fences down, but the house still stood, lonely and decayed, with burdock and milkweed fouling the dooryard, and the privy overturned. He saw no one, but there was fresh laundry hanging from a line: a man's trousers, which he recognized as the water saint's, and a shirt and some women's shifts.

He said everything was burned thereabouts but for the church and sundry forts where the people repaired when raiders were on hand. He said the land was wasted and everything smelled of smoke and rotting bodies (he himself smelled to me of smoke, as though it had permeated his skin or as though he were on fire somewhere, smoldering). His hand clutched at his tomahawk the whole time we spoke as if he were debating whether to attack me. And likewise I was ready to strike him down—for love, I think, so contrary an emotion love is.

He was so distant from me in mind, so full of hatred, I could not bear it and would rather have had him dead. Joseph Brant has a son, too, who hates him. This is a puzzle. Brant's son drinks and runs from a fight and sits at campfire plotting the most amaz-ing revenges against his father for betraying his people. Tom Wopat told me that one day Brant will kill the boy like a dog. Will I kill Oskar? I wonder.

I remember holding him as a baby. His first night on earth he slept on my chest, grappling at my chest hair, while Margrethe dozed and cried out. (When she was awake, she would scream, "Air ye satisfied? Well, air ye satisfied?" Her screams nigh wrenched the hair from my head.)

To Thee Whose Voice Is Great We Pray (from Oskar's Book about Indians)

It is gestures (words) that use us as their instruments, as their bearers and incarnations. Scholars, philologists, etymologists, and Indianologists (see Lafitau et al.) agree that the Iroquois sacred language contains words of ancient origin, the meanings of which are little understood even by the Indians themselves. Nevertheless the Indians view the repetition of these words in ceremonies as absolutely crucial to their ritual efficacy.

When I asked him about the song he taught me, Tom Wopat said that we will be made new only when we learn to speak the language we cannot understand. He said our bodies are made up of a million million suns—flesh made up of suns. Did he mean this as metaphor, analogy, or scientific hypothesis? Did he mean that all languages which are foreign are sacred? Did he mean that difference itself is sacred? That my savior is the other, whoever he is?

I believe now that my father's downfall was in taking an aesthetic rather than a moral view of life.

This is one of the reasons he loved Indians.

The difficulty of writing a book about Indians is akin (or analogous) to the difficulty Indian Department officers like my father had in holding the Indians in readiness for a prolonged war. The Indians were always electing new leaders or fracturing into any number of smaller parties, going off on hunts, taking time out on the march to practice their uncanny rituals, falling into panics because of a sign, or simply going home because they felt like it. Organized, they were untrustworthy and indifferent troops; on their own, they were astonishing and terrible.

What does this mean? To remain true to themselves, the Indians had to lose; to survive, they had to forget.

The other side had reason, history, and the individual—those great and wonderful European inventions (fictions).

The book about Indians can't be a book at all. (As a book, I agree, it's a mess, no substitute for all the histories, geographies, anthropologies, and novels that will one day illuminate the subject of Indians.) It is a song, a hymn, a keen, a cry of mourning and condolence. It is a recitation of names, a string of masks, a prayer. It is a break, a rupture in the whole cloth of normal discourse. It is an antibook meant to destroy all books. It is pure ritual, mumbo jumbo, words of power, a spell—not to be read as a book at all, but to be incanted over and over until it infects the soul, until the words pierce the skull and suck out the brain, until the brain is turned upside down.

If you read the book carefully enough, it will change your life.

If you read the book the correct way, you will become an Indian (that is what I intend; that is the purpose of all books that are not books).

The Iroquois name for God is He Whose Voice Is Great, or, more literally, Big Words.

World without end, All Men.

The Down-fended Boy

That night, or one such night, or a night in some completely other century or universe—it is all the same to Oskar—they lie up in the rock cave beneath Anthony's Nose. By the flickering firelight, Oskar believes he begins to recognize some of the ancient wall paintings. No one has told him what they mean, but he is in a fever from his wounds (mostly accidental or self-inflicted) and drifts in and out of dreams, and the paintings begin to inhabit his dreams.

Are you ready to write? he thinks. Are you ready to tell the truth?

In his dream, he is the good brother, Sapling. After a terrible struggle, he kills the Great Water Serpent, the Fire Dragon of the White Body, with a goose-quill pen given him by his father.

Oskar has never heard of the Fire Dragon.

When Oskar wakes, Tom Wopat is playing a water drum, singing to a row of masks. The Seneca boy, Handsome Lake, lies dead drunk on a rock shelf beneath the paintings. His breath bubbles in and out like water. The cave smells of vomit. In the firelight, with the drum throbbing, the paintings seem to move, to dance, upon the walls.

Oskar carefully unfolds and presses flat a sheet of paper stolen from the last settlement they raided. Before their attack, it had been used to wrap meat. The Indians took it for musket wadding. But Oskar wants to write. He has good ink—the widder gave it to him as a going-away present. On the back of the bloody page there is a letter scribbled in thin, fading ink. It begins: "dear Genl. Washington, I went to Deygart's (you remember I said he was Chairman of the Committee of Public safety . . .)"

Oskar writes: "on the March Yesternight, tom Wopat said he must Dy soon. It wracked my Heart to hear & at first I would Not believe him. He said he must go feed the Iroquois God of War, Agreskwe, wch means in English 'The Reason or Cause of Absence.'

"He said I would remove to Canada, that Handsome Lake w'd stop drinking & save the Remnant of his People, & that Agreskwe called him.

"He told me this Story—how he was born to a Mohawk Girl

without a Husband. How he came before his Time & would not cry & the savage Midwives believ'd he would die before Dawn. They put him Naked outside the Lodge in a Bank of Snow & tended his Mother. But ere long the poor Woman let out a sudden Discharge of Blood & gave up the Ghost screaming her Lover's Name wch was afterward kept Secret.

"In the Morning, one of the Midwives went to Piss & returned babbling that the Baby lived Yet. When they went to look, they Severally noted that tom had terrible Black Eyes wch seem'd to glow & made nary a Sound, only looked & looked & breathed in stopping Gasps. The Snow round about him was turned to Ice.

"A Medicine Woman named Sail bade them build a tiny Elm-Bark Lodge. She strewed it all about with Down from cattail Spikes so no Person could disturb the Child unbeknownst & in this Manner she kept him apart for twelve Years. In that Time, nary a Live person saw tom Wopat save for Sail, & he himself only went abroad at Night.

"This down-fending is an ancient Custom not much practiced these days. It was, in former Times, a Sign of Fear & Respect for a Child considered werrie powerful in Magic. (I ne'er saw any Evidence of this with tom, tho he has allays been Extremely odd. Also he can read as well as Dominie Frederici.)

"At twelve, he says, he escaped from Sail who had grown quite Blind & would fall asleep at Times—when she was squatting to make Water or in the Middle of a Sentence (oncet tom had to pull her from the Fire into wch she had fallen). He went across the River to live among the White People & go about in Daylight (tho his Eyes are sensitive yet). The Jester, Witcacy, took him in.

"The Mohawk call him the down-fended Boy. They fear & revere Him. He is the Fatherless Child, the one who lives between Worlds. Later my Father gave him the green-glass Spectacles on account of his sore Eyes."

When he is finished writing, Oskar consigns the words to the fire.

*   *   *

He sleeps again and dreams of a princess sleeping by a lake with a sow bear standing guard. A lion swims by, diving for fish, throwing up huge waves when it goes under, swamping little boats along the shore. An army of scarecrow soldiers marches along the beach. They are starved thin, their clothes stained with soil and sweat, their weapons red with rust. Many are wounded and need help from their fellows to make their way. Somehow, from the sad expressions on the soldiers' faces, Oskar knows that they are all already dead. This is Agreskwe's army, the legion of the dead.

When Oskar wakes up, his head no longer aches. But he is fierce with knowledge. He also has an erection. He touches himself and thinks of Beatrice Weiderpris. Beatrice, he imagines, would gasp when he entered her, and scream and pound his back with her fat, white fists. She would protest and acquiesce, struggle and surrender, in an endless cycle of resistance and satisfaction.

But the image of Beatrice no longer arouses him, and his penis wilts. He remembers the widder, the legion of widders left by the war, and the apparition of the girl lifting her shift in the moonlight.

I will never see Beatrice Weiderpris, he thinks.

He cannot imagine now that he ever loved her. For the widder has taught him some secret about pity and loss, which are the gentler components of love.

Tom Wopat, boiling tea and sugar at the fire, hands him a tin cup, and Oskar, looking up, sees his own painted face reflected upside down in the spectacles.

A Time of Prophets and Prophecies

All the same, I knew Scattering Light was dead upon the trail somewhere in the future, somewhere far away, and that Approaching Thunder would bring me back his head in some confused Messessagey desire to make me feel better.

I was in the middle of a long journey. I did not know where

I was going or whence I had come. I was a falling stone. The world had turned itself upside down for me. I was an Indian, though pale, and a white woman, though I spoke and walked like an Indian. For the sake of my lover, I wished all white men dead. But sometimes I dreamed sad dreams of Mam and Pap and wished for a baby like little Orvis.

Was Pap a-hunting for me? Did my redeemer live? Was I wandering in the wilderness or had I been saved? Had I already met the Head-Piercer in the shape of Scattering Light? Whence came these strange thoughts to me?

Two boys, Bekwinabi, or He Who Sits in a Treetop, and Awan, or Fog, returned from a summer hunt with tales of a white settlement a-building on Messessagey land west of the river, farms sprouting on the Indian prairie opposite Fort Niagara, cattle and hogs roaming in the woods. It made the Real People anxious to hear. For them also, the world seemed suddenly strange.

With the men all gone to war, it was a summer of women, usually a time of games and dancing and endless gossip. But that summer it rained a lot, and we spent long days in the lodges doing the cat's cradle, our eyes tearing with smoke. And the women going about their daily work felt watched, though when they looked or thought about it they could not say why.

One day an albino Leni-Lenape (the Nottaways called them women, though no one knew why, and they resented it considerably) appeared, painted red and black and dressed in a fire-red trade blanket, eagle feathers dyed red, and his tattoos—nothing more (and his tattoos were like bones; he had a face like a skull). He was a Christian convert and a preacher and mad, probably. When he spoke, he foretold the end of the world in a fiery cloud. He had a piece of buckskin, folded small, with a map and some figures on it, which he said was called the Great Book, or Writing. In that book was written the fate of all the Indians.

He opened his blanket like a pair of great scarlet wings—with that strange, pale skull face between—and said God (he called Him Gitche-manido, the Great Spirit, who is one of the Grandfathers) would redeem the good Christians from the fire while all the rest would be consumed, not once but over and over without any end. (For Indians, these were the fevered, last days of wandering prophets and prophecies—some of this I recalled from Dominie Frederici's thundering sermons, though now and in my memory it made as little sense.)

The Messessagey treated him politely (they are afraid that any stranger might be a manido or magician in disguise, and beneath the paint he looked white or, rather, not quite white, which was worse—with that book and all, he was something in between), fed him, and then asked him to leave. If he didn't leave, they said they would kill him and eat his heart.

Later, I heard or dreamed that the Leni-Lenape prophet met two raggedy white traders from the old French fort at Toronto. The traders made him drunk on watered brandy and then bet him a small keg he wouldn't shoot himself in the head. The Leni-Lenape took a pistol from the trader, cocked it, and shot himself dead through the eye, laughing.

A.T.'s wife, Waboonasay, had gotten over the jealousy she felt on account of my staying with Wabanooqua and was a-teaching me to cook the Messessagey way. (Later, every last one of my husbands complained of my cooking—this is why.)

Waboonasay was full of Messessagey advice, some'at the way Aunt Annie had been full of old German superstition. Mostly I ignored it (though later in life I remembered everything, remembered the monotonous softness of her voice, the doughy heaviness of her fat forearm, and the words). She had more wabeno lore (to hear her talk) than Wabanooqua and was allays a-telling me to walk eight times around a mugwort plant and face east afore taking a leaf for my bag. She warned me that Wabanooqua had round heels and went around seducing men half her age despite her ugliness. One of these days a manido would catch up with her and turn her into a rock.

One night Waboonasay gave me an old bear's bladder stuffed stiff with moss. She said it was a love medicine. I should use it when I was lonely for Scattering Light. She found herself that she preferred a bear's bladder to Approaching Thunder even when he was around.

I still have the bear's bladder, shriveled and black, with a fine dry powder of moss dust inside, but I ain't nary used it oncet (though Oskar tried to make me).

Waboonasay said I could even try making love to one of the younger boys scampering about the camp playing Indians against the Bostons or Messessageys against the Nottaways. These boys would stop their play from time to time and ask me questions while I tried to master quill and bead work (my thumbs were a mass of festering sores after an afternoon of this).

Was it true white people came from Nanebojo's turds?

Was it true their tongues were shaped so they couldn't bend them around Indian words?

Were white people smarter than dogs, beavers, horses?

Did white people shit like Indians?

Was it true that white people ate Indians?

Did white men have smaller penises than Indian men?

These questions sometimes made me laugh, sometimes made me sad, for they reminded me that oncet I was not a Messessagey. And later, when I knew the worst, I did go into the bushes with one or two of the little laughing boys (Fog and one whose name I forgot). But they are all dead now.

An Anatomy of War

The Rebel colonel Brown is dead and a hero, a dead hero, shot through the thighs. We massacre him and a hundred militia at the Noses (on our side, we lose three Indians; Joseph is wounded in the foot). It is a pretty fight. It is a minuet of death.

Three deserters from our side slip away in the night to warn Brown at Stein Araby that our command is split on two sides of the river. Thinking to catch us so, he rushes his troops down the

cart road in the dark. But Joseph Brant spied the traitors departing, and the bulk of our army crosses the Mohawk River at Spraker's Drift and hides among the trees ere dawn.

At first light, we send our Indians (and my son) across a
corn stubble field in a fog to pin Brown's men behind a log fence,
and then unleash Butler's Rangers and the English regulars on
the flanks. The savages rush shrieking into a fog of death. Oskar
rushes shrieking into a fog of death. I don't know if he is brave
or crazy.

When the carnage is through, my Messessageys stroll
amongst the bodies, picking up weapons and slaughtering the
wounded. They find a headless corpse, dressed for a gentleman,
with an epic of tattoos on its body skin.

I recognize the tattoos.

I kneel next to the body and try to say a prayer.

I say, "Lord, take thy servant Tom . . ."

But I have no prayer in me. I am numb. Even my headache
disappears. I think only that I must get back to the arms of Alice
Kissane and bury my face in her breast or I will myself expire
from too much loss.

The Rebel colonel Brown is dead and a hero, a dead hero, shot
through the thighs. We massacre him and a hundred militia at
the Noses. But his dead have done their work (it is the job of any
soldier to die usefully). Before the last shots, General Van Rensselaer's advance guard appears on the south bank of the river.

The general has 1,500 men, including two regiments of Continentals and a hundred traitor Oneidas. (For the Indians, as with
us, it is brother against brother, uncle against uncle. This war has
split their confederacy forever, and, though something new is being born yonder, it is a monster to us.) They are so aghast at the
cut-up condition of Brown's command that, instead of pinning us
between the two forces, they stop to consult, which gives us time
to break off and chase upriver, burning the farms on either side
so that a column of smoke darkens the sky at our backs.

Three miles upriver we pass the little Caroga Creek with Fox's mill burned to a black skeleton and the stone church with the bronze cock upon the steeple, which remains untouched out of respect for me. When we reach my former home, I fall out with Wabecamegot and Hole in the Sky and tether Miehlke by the stable door. I kick aside the burst door and step inside the house for the first time in four years. No one is about, but the bed is made and a framed silhouette of Margrethe's mother lies upon the table, feathered with dust. I feel like a ghost or a shadow, as the Messessagey call it. My heart says, Everything is so familiar but dead. Or perhaps this is only the way the real world looks to a dead man.

As I walk about inside, my son comes to stand in the doorway, leaning upon the jamb, looking more savage than the savages. He has two Charleville muskets and a bag of False Face masks over his shoulder, which he retrieved from Tom Wopat's pack. He wears a pair of green-glass spectacles with one glass starred by a bullet fragment. The frames are loose, and he keeps pushing them up on his nose with his forefinger, staring at me with eyes I cannot see. His face is divided down the middle and painted like an Indian's.

He has become something other than my son. What he thinks I have no idea. He is a mystery to me, as I am to myself. But I believe he must be grateful I loved him and beat him, for I made him strong.

When I turn my back on the house, I hear the click-click-snap of a musket lock. For an instant, I think Oskar is shooting me. I believe briefly (thankfully) that I am about to die in my own dooryard. But there is no report. A catbird sings mockingly in the lilacs by the privy. Oskar is kneeling at the stoop, using his musket flint and pan to light the dry grass in the yard. When it flames up, he gathers a handful and uses it as a torch. Before I can shout no, the flames are licking up the walls.

He stands so close, looking into the heart of the blazing house, that I think he must be scorched or that the powder in his horn will go off. But he calmly watches till the roof caves in, then gathers his muskets and bag of faces and returns to his company of young Iroquois fighters.

The whole thing gives me a headache.

I have clutched a mad dog to my bosom.

I think, kidnapping him, I redeemed him from history and democracy. For what? So that he could threaten me, turn Indian, and burn down my house?

If I bleed myself again this week, I'll die.

Just past my former home, we take fire from a fortified farm lying close to the road. We see Van Rensselaer's militia racing along the south bank of the river to head us off at the next ford (some are old friends—men wave and shout family news back and forth) so we have no time to reduce the building. Instead we turn inland briefly, leaving the strong point and threading our way through the fields and woods to pick up the road beyond.

But already we realize that we are late. By Grandfather Klock's house a line of Rebels is forming, growing stronger at every moment as fresh troops wade across the river. (Let me tell you, it is a strange thing to fight a war over ground where you played foxes and hounds as a boy and courted your wife and watched your children tumble in the hayricks.)

I espy Oskar with the Indians. I can only distinguish him by the bag slung over his shoulder and the glint of the glass spectacles in the declining sunlight. He races up the hill like a flame of light, preceding the Indians by half a dozen yards, his mouth gaping in a scream. The Americans fire a volley straight on, but he continues without abatement. He does not shoot his musket but swings it like a club, whirling in the sunset, laying out Rebels on either side. Once or twice he lays out an Indian too by mistake.

When the Americans see it, they recoil. Their line begins to fold. There ain't but a couple of hundred loyal Indians and most of them pause to reload and shoot up the hill. But all at once the Americans start running. We raise a shout, which is premature. (Actually, the English raise a shout. They yell, "God save the

King," which irritates me no end because of my head. I count too many kin upon that hill and inside old Klock's stronghold. Everywhere is the dark nubbin of chaos and doubt. All is whirl. We are children of the whirlwind.)

Van Rensselaer has a field gun posted in an embrasure in the stone fence round Klock's apple orchard (where the stile used to be—I once hooked up Henrietta Switt's skirt and saw her fanny going over that stile). The gun fires. The Americans turn at the wall, under cover of the gun and the farmers hidden inside. They re-form their line and calmly begin to pick off Indians. (This too is new, this resolve, which leads to battles that go to and fro and are not all one way.) When the Indians run back down the hill because of the artillery, the Americans think we are broken and charge.

But we are not broken, and the savages simply melt through our formation and disappear behind. We counter with fierce volley fire along the line. Van Rensselaer calls a retreat, and we duck into the woods on our flank.

The Indians lead us all night on their old hunting trails. Consequently we get lost, and the army breaks up into eight smaller parties. It takes days to get everyone back together again, and we nearly lose the boats and supplies on Wood Creek to the enemy. At the rendezvous, a Mohawk paddler brings news of Ferguson's defeat at King's Mountain in the Carolinas. Nine hundred Watauga mountain men, each with nothing more than a horse, a Deckhard rifle, and a bag of dried corn, have massacred a thousand Tories and shocked Cornwallis into a premature winter camp at Winnsboro.

Despite getting lost, our men have been noisy with success until the word gets out. Once more all our blood and terror have gone for nothing, canceled out by events a thousand miles away. When they hear it, the men grow silent or scoff or begin to whisper of farming in Canada.

(This is a great divide, I think. This is the place where the Rebels leave everything behind and turn their footsteps toward a bright and shining future. Whereas we, on our side, rehitch our dreary loads and trudge onward as before.

I think, They are remaking themselves, while we remain the same—though also we are altered merely by looking on, altered in the way of bitterness and envy.)

Mindless of the danger, I nick a vein with the scolper and let the blood flow till I black out. The darkness is friendly. It leads west. When I wake up, I find savage bandages and poultices strapped to my legs. The Messessageys have conducted me to Fort Niagara. She Walks the Sky has saved my life.

Turning the Brain Upside Down
(from Oskar's Book about Indians)

I recall a strange coincidence (the truth of which is now lost by virtue of this garbled transliteration) when, at the turning of the year 1779, the Seneca tried to resurrect an ancient rite called the Feast of Fools or Turning the Brain Upside Down (now little known or understood even by them—one day this will be the only record of the rite, and the descendants of savages will read it and try to reconstruct themselves out of the gray words).

They did this in a fever of anxiety, for the structure of the old was already broken, the great council fire at Onondaga extinguished, and the Tree of Peace upended.

From the Gate of the Five Nations to La Belle Famille, men and women ran out of their huts and dugouts, loosening their clothes, throwing ashes over themselves, acting out their dreams in mime, pretending they were animals or monsters. They proceeded from this to acts of fornication. Men and women committed adultery, had multiple partners, the old slept with the young.

A light snow had begun to fall. Inside the fort, the Rangers and civilians, refugees and captives redeemed from the Indians, set huge bonfires alight, and torches ringed the walls. The Gate of the Five Nations stood open. I hovered at the gate looking now inward, now outward. Inside was the civilized world compassed by the fortress walls, the guns standing guard, the strange snow warriors, now turned to ice, facing the forest and the stars. Outside the savages danced about their fires and cried and made the motions and gestures of madmen or seemed lost in a sexual frenzy.

At midnight, three red-coated drummer boys, with dirty, frayed cuffs and torn stockings, toured the parade square while a lone fifer played a march called "The World Turned Upside Down." The music echoed off the walls and went out to the forest and the stars. Somewhere beyond the fort's membrane of stone, mortar, and logs, I knew my father was cavorting with Alice Kissane. I knew too my father had been in liquor, trying to stave off a headache. Now he was staggering awkwardly in the snow, taking part in that wretched savage ritual, turning the brain upside down to make everything else come right.

In the Feast of Fools, dreams came true. When the brain was turned upside down, all the normal rules that governed relations were reversed. An Indian brave, dressed in a blue serge uniform coat with silver lace at the cuffs, bangles and white beads braided into his scalp lock, his face smeared red, a fusil hanging at his shoulder, ran up and demanded the hanger I used for a sword.

He said, "Brother, I dreamed thee gave me thy blade that I might wash it in the blood of a Boston."

His aspect was so menacing that I handed over the hanger with alacrity, and the warrior disappeared in a swirl of new snow.

The world turned upside down.

Turning the brain upside down.

The coincidence of words made me suddenly feel that the words themselves had a structure and a destiny apart from their human uses.

Or that the words used me.

The Keeper of Faces Goes West

On the day of his death, Tom Wopat dresses like a gentleman: ruffled shirt, white silk stockings, stocks at the neck, a speckled waistcoat, skintight breeches, and a full beaver hat. He wears new riding boots on his feet and carries a riding crop instead of a gun or a knife (though they ate his little horse, Pell-Mell, in March when a late winter storm caught them on the trail). His hair is tied in a queue at the back and powdered. He is wearing his green-glass spectacles.

It makes Oskar angry to see. Beneath the clothes, Oskar knows, Tom Wopat is a seething riot of tattoos, maps, and diagrams. Underneath the clothes, Tom bears the whole mystical history of his race.

Oskar himself has never looked that good, never worn such boots. His own hair is chopped off at the sides with a bristling centerline rising like a crest and falling behind like a horse's tail. Seven or eight different kinds of insects live in it. He scratches an itch or a bite somewhere on his body every idle moment. He's wearing beaded moccasins worn paper-thin, a breechclout, and deer-hide leggings, torn and stained from months in the woods. A bone chest plate hangs in front and rattles when he walks. His face is painted, red on one side, black on the other.

He carries a hanger, a scolper, and an iron pipe tomahawk strapped on a shoulder belt, and two French .69-caliber Charleville muskets with their barrels cut down for easy handling in the brush. He has loaded the muskets with balls so tight he has to pound them in with the tomahawk and three buckshot on top of the balls.

When he stands still, he falls asleep from fear and fatigue.

But getting mad at Tom Wopat keeps him awake.

*   *   *

Three hundred and fifty Americans, mostly militia from Johns-town and Stein Araby, with a handful of Continentals for back-bone, lie hidden away behind a log fence across a corn stubble field. Oskar can't see the Americans or the fence or even the corn stubble field because of the thick morning fog. He knows they are there because Handsome Lake and Tom Wopat spotted three horsemen scouting at dawn and followed them as far as the fence.

Oskar has maybe four dozen Indians and two private soldiers from the King's 8th Foot manning a three-pounder field gun they call a grasshopper, mounted on a sled with wooden skids. The English privates have stripped off their red coats and shout "Damn 'ee! Damn 'ee!" over and over as they try to puzzle out how much powder to put in the gun and how to point it.

The Indians laze about on the grass, freshening their face paint, clutching their medicine bags, singing little war songs. A Christian Mohawk from Montreal says his rosary in the tall grass.

Every sound carries on the damp air. They can hear the Americans shouting orders and clanging their shovels and bayo-nets against rocks as they dig their rifle pits.

"Damn 'ee!" shout the privates. "Damn 'ee!"

A mourning dove begins to coo in a basswood tree.

Seating himself cross-legged at a freshly sawed stump, Oskar writes hastily on a torn sheet of newspaper (he found it in the hole beneath an overturned privy, crumpled and caked with old shit, which he scraped off with his scolper): "Der Gen'l Washing-ton, I take this Opportunity wch will probably be my Last to Pen you a lettre (I pray it will be discovered on my Corps when the Battle is o'er) as of Old by Way of Xplaining my Thoughts & Actions of Late. I am no Doubt a Mystery to You as I am to Myself. But I b'lieve you are the Perfect Father—next to my Own Imperfect One—& will understand.

"Later I am to lead my Savages directly against Colonel Brown's militia wch has come down hoping to catch us divided with the River between. But the Tories waded across Spraker's Drift by the Little Nose at Dawn & hid so that Colonel Brown marches toward a Trap. My Savages are the Bait.

"Tom Wopat says there will be a Carnage and that he him-self will Dy. This is too much for me to bear. He is my oldest Friend even if he is an Indian. (He is my Shadow, my Dark Twin, but always ahead of me in Brains as if he come out of Ma first. I could ne'er catch up.) I am going to Slaughter Americans, my former Allies, yer Friends. This does not upset me as much as you might think.

"Lately, I have had some Inkling of the True Meaning of my History. It came to me Yesternight when I passed ye Church with the Bronze Cock where my Mother is buried. I set beside her Grave an Hour a-missing her, or maybe missing the good Mother she weren't in Life. (She & my Father fell in Love once over a yeller Dog wch is more Love than I will ever Enjoy—even if, as I believe, they were completely mistaken about One another.) I be-lieve she a-spoke to me, or maybe it was the Wind. She said I was a Fool & had no Luck & would end up in Canada one Day Defeated & Envious. She said I would always understand Things too late & see Life at a Distance. She said my Real Name was Almost but that weren't no Name for a Man. I went away after that because she sounded too much like herself.

"Witcacy, the Dwarf, has come in riding a poled Cow with a saddle & a scabby udder, leading his Negro Wench & carrying a Book of Ancient Rhetoric wch he saved when the Militia burned his House. Because they burned his House, he says he must be a Tory & will go to Niagara with us when we have scorched Every-thing. He says he saw Beatrice Weiderpris with a Man named Wim-ple who Sir William Johnson once saved from being Gaoled for Debt. Her Husband Weiderpris is Dead but his Estate went under the Act of Attainder & she is Penniless. Wimple is Caretaker of Johnson Hall & eats off Johnson's Plate & makes Beatrice drag a Plow in the Garden for Lack of a Horse. Witcacy says she is Fat & dotes on Wimple & shouts when she comes so Loud that All the Neighbors hear it. He says she is Stupid & cannot read.

"He thinks I look well as an Indian. This makes me uncom-mon Proud, tho' I cannot explain why.

"This War has turned my Brain upside down. That wch I loved I hate & that wch I oncet hated I love. Such Inconstancy is a Sin. I well remember my Oath to the Committee & Congress. Perhaps the Truth is that I am already Dead & in Hell & these we call Savages are Imps & Devils as my Grandma Klock always used to Say.

"I must tell you they are about me now, naked, combing their Hair as the Spartans once did before giving Battle. They wish a beautiful Death as do I (I amn't much good at anything Else).

"Yer Correspondent in the Underworld.

"Oskar Nellis."

Oskar's father brings a message. It says, "Perform ye miracles."

The savages are a line of faces disappearing into the fog. When Oskar gives a yell, they yell back. He does this out of bravado, to impress his father. In the midst of his terror, he feels a shudder of pride. Oh, he thinks, there is nothing like leading painted men into a fog of death. Oh, he thinks, this glimmer of a feeling is my New Jerusalem, or as close as I'll ever get.

And at least I ain't a virgin.

Hendrick's eyes are red and rheumy. There is a long stab of a cut down the middle of his forehead. When he takes a step, his boots squelch. He looks pale, as though he had no blood in him. He looks as though he is shrinking, getting older before Oskar's eyes. And he barely notices his son, but talks.

"Lad," he says, "have ye made a will?"

"No."

"It's good to leave things tidy."

Hendrick scratches his beard, catching a louse between his thumbnail and forefinger.

"D' ye still write letters?" Hendrick asks. "Yer mother wanted to learn to write, but her fingers were stubby and clumsy and she could not form her ABCs. Oncet she asked Sir William Johnson's Irish cousin, Warren, to learn her when she saw him writing his diary. He put his hand up her dress and she went about crying that she was pregnant. All her troubles began with embarrassment."

Hendrick suddenly looks over at the grasshopper gun, an expression of sharp inquiry etched on his features.

"Don't let them shoot that thing. Mark me, they'll run the shot up your backs in a charge. Can you believe they captured half the world with soldiers like that? I think I will have a word with Tom yonder."

Oskar's own face is red and black, divided down the middle, like a Whirlwind mask. When his father turns away, Oskar clasps his arms around a tree for fear then breaks away with a gasp and runs screaming into the cloud.

Oskar is suddenly alone in the cornfield, running. American musket balls fill the air with a high humming sound (coming out of the barrel, the balls change shape, elongate or splinter, and the pieces fly end over end getting ready to tear up flesh).

When the Indians, leaping out of the fog like an army of ghosts, reach the line fence, the Americans stand up and fire a volley, and the whole attack collapses in an instant, the Indians ducking low and stepping back into the mist. Oskar meditates a moment by the fence, irritated as usual with their lack of resolve. Also relieved. He wraps his letter around a rock and flings it toward the Americans. Someone on the other side shouts, "Be-damn!" in protest.

Retreating a few yards, Oskar gathers his Indians behind a stump pile where they light their pipes and count heads. No one is hit. In other parts of the battlefield, they hear the sound of the Rangers and Royal Greens closing with the American flanks. They fire a ragged volley blind toward the Americans to hold their center, then Oskar gives the word to fall back.

At the edge of the field, the English privates set a match to their gun. There is a strange slapping thunk, and Tom Wopat seems to leap backward into the air, falling on his rear with his legs over his head.

Only he hasn't got a head.

And he is carrying his green-glass spectacles in his hand.

Oh, It Is Bitter

Now it was dead (or dying). I had never seen a tree so moribund. There weren't nary a leaf left on it. Its roots had rotted off. It looked like a skeleton. Someone, maybe an angry manido, had knocked the top off during the night.

(My song predicted it.

In a vision I saw it.

Scattering Light was dead or dying—in some blood-spattered glade.

How did I know?

The world was a-shouting it at me in a thousand ways.

I hated the world.)

I cried so much at night, my arms wrapped around Red Dog's neck, that Wabanooqua finally made me move out of our hutment. She said her sleep was more important than mourning for some man.

She had become moody of late. She was seeing ugly things in the future. She was seeing the dying of her race and a day when they would not even speak their own language any longer. (Lately, Wabanooqua had been dreaming A.T.'s dream. She said she wisht he would keep his dreams to himself.)

Our separate mournings and obsequies were boring and irritating to the other like separate vivid dreams.

I went and talked to the dead tree (Scattering Light). I preached whole sermons of loss to it. When Red Dog ran off for a piss in the woods or after a rabbit, I would run screaming through the whole camp a-searching for him, thinking he was lost for good. I dreamed at night in nightmares, remembering the whole violent beginning of my life amongst the savages. The silent coming, Abiel's quiet sniffling over his guts, Philomena's screams, Baby Orvis tugging at my dry, flat nipple and the sight of him arcing bloodily in the sunlight. (Somehow I had never remembered this so vividly. Somehow part of me had decided to forget that it was the Messessagey who had done this to my family. Remembering, I began to hate the Indians ever so little in my heart. Remembering, I prepared myself for separation. Remembering, I cut myself off always from the present from then on. I was a witness, but could never participate in events, feelings, emotions.)

Oh, it was bitter, but it was my life.

I thought, My name is Mary Hunsacker (then I remembered Scattering Light's snake head and went off on a whole other dream).

A moon later, when the frost was in the ground, Approaching Thunder brought me my lover's heart and head and eight American scalps (none familiar) in a sack, which gesture he thought would somehow console me.

It did not.

I ate the heart.

A.T. said if I did this I might use my powers to go west and retrieve Scattering Light from Nanebojo's country. He said the Head-Piercer would recognize me and not trouble to take my brain a second time. But in my dreams, west was a direction I could never find.

Scattering Light's face was brasted. It looked as if it had been cooked in a pot. His nose was gone. (Later, I lost the head along with a new pair of moccasins, my sewing kit, a beaded sash, and two thin chickens fording Big Creek during the spring runoff.)

Approaching Thunder said the militia had caught the Loyalists in a field hard by Fort Klock.

Was my father there?

Had he taken a shot at my lover?

Had they met in some secluded corner of the battlefield and somehow recognized one another in the smoke and thunder?

On the whole, I thought, probably not.

(Though I dreamed continuously and believed my dreams like the Messessagey, I remained something of a realist. Living between two worlds, I saw them both more clearly than anyone on the inside. I was a machine for translation—which is a kind of prophecy—though no one used me.)

In the ensuing fight, Scattering Light's trade musket had burned his nose off when it vented flame from the touchhole.

For three days, they had led my blind, smoldering lover through rebel Oneida country with naught to eat but their leggings boiled in a pot. A.T.'s hunting skills (as usual) completely abandoned him in that alien land. Though Scattering Light didn't eat none anyway. He was a-singing his death song, which to the others sounded like a constant whispered lament.

At night, his face glowed and sent up little spurts of flame (from the hot black powder embedded in his flesh).

During the day, smoke came off him.

He was a living dead man, pain with legs, a whispering, singing agony. I wisht they'd have kilt him earlier than later. And when they did, he kicked and kicked while A.T. drew a scolper round his throat. A.T. said sadly it was the most graceless death he had ever witnessed, which made me angry to hear.

I knew Scattering Light weren't a coward. It was love that made him struggle so, love and wanting not to say good-bye.

Makatawanikwapun Kwawisiwawitikamakwipun.

I wish to marry a black-haired girl.

After this I was inconsolable and a considerable discomfort to the Messessagey, who believed that I was turning into (a) a windigo or (b) a witch. Either way, some wanted to kill me. Wabanooqua said it was my white side to speak always of love and loss and go to such extremes of mourning.

(At this time, I began to grow fat from sucking maple-sugar

candy all the time. And I started to twist out strands of my hair, one after the other, till there was a little bald patch at the back of my head.)

Makatawanikwapun Kwawisiwawitikamakwipun.

I wish to marry . . .

(He dies. He dies.)

Field of Bones

October–November 1781

In the Shadowlands

*O*skar adjusts the dirty eighteen-tailed surgical bandage below his knee, uses the tip of a broken ramrod to scratch the scab beneath the dressing. Two lengths of maple kindling strapped on either side form a rough splint.

Field dressing, Dr. McCausland called it.

Lightning flickers eerily in the blackened trees beyond the little clearing by the river. A cold winter rain thunders against the bulging canvas sheet where the roof should be. It streams down inside the freshly cut logs of the cabin wall. It spatters the curling elm-bark sheets strewn over the corn-husk mattress where Oskar lies, his head propped against a saddle. He pulls his damp bedclothes more tightly about his shoulders, scrapes the candle wax down with his knife so the flame burns higher, and bends to his work, scratching at the scrolls with the stub of a hardwood twig charred black in the fire.

Are you ready to write? he thinks.

Are you ready to tell the truth?

Are you ready?

He writes: "My dear Gen'l Washington, I have the honor to inform you of my imminent Death by Gun Shot rec'd from my own Cousin, Milo Nellis, the Family Historian (pardon if I sound bitter), when Col Marinus Willet pinned us in the snowy Woods at Johnstown last Month. (Please do not give Milo a Medal whatever he says. I recognized him & stood up to shake his Hande when he drew down on me with his Musket at Fifteen Paces & near blew my Leg off.) Dr McCausland of the King's 8th Ret/d said he must take the Leg but I refused.

"I write the Above on an Elm Bark Scroll with a Charcoal Stick & put it with the Others.

"Yrs. in Hell (Canada) Oskar."

Under his blankets, Oskar wears a linsey-woolsey shirt, an unraveling sweater Mary Hunsacker knitted for him, a pair of deerskin breeches, mismatched stockings, much darned about the heels and toes, and moccasins badly sewn in the Messessagey fashion. His scalp lock has escaped its queue and flies out over his ears like wings. Beneath his shirt, his body is quilted with tattoos—spirals and winged serpents, stylized male and female genitalia, fabulous beasts with human heads and legs, lines and animal tracks.

(After the battle at the Noses, Oskar lost himself in a delirium of writing. He wrote on roster sheets, requisition forms, old letters, newspapers, and pages torn from books. He wrote in the sand with his big toe. He wrote words when he pissed in the snow. He wrote with water on the tip of his finger and called it invisible ink. He wrote in the air. He stole whitewash from the quartermaster stores at Fort Niagara and painted messages on the walls, on rock outcrops along Indian paths, on ships' hulls, and tree trunks. Once he painted a sentence on a cow; another time he penned a phrase on the withers of the colonel's horse before she kicked him. He burned messages into planks with his bayonet point and floated them down rivers. He wrote over the words he'd already written till there was nothing but a confused, spidery exfoliation of incomprehensible text.

He could not abide a blank space.

During the winter, he hired a German jaeger named Hans Frelicher with a talent for freehand drawing to give him a tattoo. One thing led to another. On his feet, he carries the words "LEFT" and "RIGHT." Over his heart, "HEART." Over his liver, "LIVER." Above his penis, "SNAKE." On his right forearm, "WIDDER-MAKER." He calls this the naming of parts.

Working from memory, he drew sketches of the designs on Tom Wopat's body and had them traced upon his own. Over his left breast is a tiny mask, split down the middle, half-blue, half-white. Nowadays, he rarely goes without his shirt.)

Are you ready to write? he thinks to himself.

Are you ready?

Oskar scratches a line beneath the words and begins again. "In the Spring my Father abandoned the War in Disgust & crossed the River Ice into Canada (a Thing he oncet swore he w'ld Never do) & started a new Country. He said he & She Walks the Sky were the New Adam & the New Eve & that their Childers would be the first in the Nation, a new Race. But he was so Weak I had to go & help him on & off his Horse. He said he was not a Tory any longer, but not a Rebel either. He wanted to live with Indians because they were the onliest People he could abide or could abide Him. (The Messessagey entreated him to come & live with them.) He is a Double Traitor."

Oskar stops and scratches another line and probes a scar in the palm of his hand with the carbonized tip of his crude pencil.

"I took to Drink on account of I could not bear to think on this & the Consequences I suffered for his Violent & Mercurial Beliefs wch was Evidence of a deep Madness. I believe I was the only Sane person West of Philadelphia despite my Tattoos, my Insomnia, my Faints & Syncopes, my Constant Drunkennes, my Morning Tears & my nervous Habit of discharging Firearms for no Reason. (Twicet I nearly drowned falling into Cart Ruts except Handsome Lake turned my Head so I could breathe. And oncet I went to sleep in a Snowbank & got frost bit on my Privy Member. I spent a Week in Prison for attacking an English Gunner with a Hatchet &, for my continued Animositie, they exiled me twice to fight Rebels in Pennsylvania & later upon the Mohawk where I received my fatal Wound—see attached Diary Excerpts.)

"There is a Girl living with my Father who once resided among the Messessagey & hath their Ways & so Wille not use the Privy. She has an Infant Dochter by a Savage & carries her Lover's Skull in a Bear's-foot Bag & hath a Silver Plate in her Forehead wch makes a Line down the Middle of her Face. She give me a Balm for my Wound wch stopped the Suppuration of Pus & relieved my Fever wch surprised her as much as it did the Doctor. She said most Things she touches dye & that my Balm was meant to inspire Love in a backwards Suitor not heal a wounded Limb—"

Hear Us, O Israel, Delivered from the Wilderness

Wabanooqua gave me a leathern strap to bite on for the pain, which I bit right through without it helping the pain at all. I told her I thought I was just putting on weight out of grief and that the pains would pass. They did not.

When it was over I had a family—a baby and a head in a bag. Luckily, the girl was hardy, for I believe myself, as with all growing things, especially plants, a fatal caretaker. (I give her an Indian name, but called her Dumpling, which was the way Mam had always addressed Baby Orvis.)

In the months that followed, I was somewhat afflicted with people wishing to save me. But I was escared of white men, remembering Indian boots and all, and took some trouble to hide my identity with frequent applications of black-walnut juice and bear grease. Wabanooqua stitched a tattoo down the center of my face (the mirror of Scattering Light's war paint, of the Redeemer he'd talked about, of the strange mask manido of my dreams) and pierced the septum of my nose with a porcupine quill from which I hung a string of relics, keepsakes, and charms. The latter dragged in my food but was especially attractive to Messessagey men, though less so as they became more and more depressed (which was the general trend).

I did not wish to be redeemed. "Redeemed" is a fancy word for rescued, saved, brought back—from what? I was happy where I was.

Not happy, miserable really. I dragged around with the baby on my back (or left her with Wabanooqua, who cosseted her) and Scattering Light's head in a bag, weeping and blowing my nose in an old moccasin.

Scattering Light is dead; oh, dead, dead is my love.

I hid mostly. I called upon my manido, my totem, the mask. I sang my song. My shadow wandered. This was the effect of my history, the blow of the death maul, my lover's death, my sojourn with Wabanooqua, my life among the savages. Even the Messessagey noticed and remarked upon it. When the Real People came to visit, to ask for medicine or advice about a witch, I was often too sad to speak.

For them my mourning was too extravagant, too white. I upset the balance of things, courting the pawaganaks and manidos, preferring their company to flesh and blood Indians. Some said I was turning into a windigo and ought to be killed. Some said I was bringing the white people onto their lands.

I had Wabanooqua's bear-paw medicine bag where I kept Scattering Light's shriveled head, but it would never speak to me. (Only fish and some shrubs talked back in those days, and I always argued with shrubs on account of their leafy nature, which I connected up with tulip trees and other such traitorous plant life.) And my dreams were more populous than my waking life.

I was playing with the dead.

I was reading the future.

I spent all my time concocting love medicines that failed to entice, cures that made my patients sicken.

But the future was as clear as creek water, and the dead were all around.

One day the Real People left me.

They moved before sunup while I was still asleep with Dumpling tucked up against my breast, took their babies and dogs. Except for Red Dog, which they judged would be too cruel.

I packed my belongings, my bits of clothing, my sewing kit and cooking pot, and my bear-foot medicine bag, and pissed on the live fire coals and went after them, weeping and carrying on and dragging my things over roots and rocks in the trail. At nightfall, I stumbled into Approaching Thunder's camp. He looked startled, though he had heard me coming a mile off. The Messessagey let me sleep by the fire and gave me samp and some chicken they had bought from a white man. But in the morning, though I had tried to sleep light and keep watch, they slipped away again.

I caught up with them the next afternoon boiling tea in pannikins over tiny fires meant to conceal their presence from the enemy. Approaching Thunder pretended he didn't see me, though I went up and stood directly before his face, my own face a mask of tears and ashes.

He said, "There are shadows about. This is not a good place to sleep. The shadows of our Grandfathers are thick as trees. I thought I just saw my dead daughter, the One Who Remembers, the one who was always predicting bad things."

That night they barely waited till I was asleep before departing.

One morning Red Dog woke me, thumping the ground about my head with his tail. A white man sat astride a tall mare at the edge of the clearing (otherwise, I was alone, though several fresh cook fires smoldered in the vicinity). I recognized him by the scar down the middle of his forehead, which made his face a twin of my own, except he had no ornaments a-dangling from his nose. He smoked a white clay pipe and rode unarmed. When he saw me looking, the Redeemer nodded. A soft moan escaped his lips, and I could see at once he was in considerable pain if not in some advanced state of physical decay (later, when he walked, I heard the blood squishing in his boots).

A-lying there, I remembered being took by Indians at age fourteen, which was my only previous experience of being ripped from the bosom of my family by a person of another race. Whatever you want to say about them, the Indians had style.

There was no one. Then they were there.

They were silent as sunlight.

I remembered Dominie Frederici thundering from the pulpit of the church with the bronze cock across the river from Fort Plank, "He hath led the Israelites out of the Wilderness into the Promised Land. He hath been a good shepherd and returned thy sheep to the fold." I wondered who the Israelites were and why white folks were so down on the wilderness anyway.

Sunlight shot between the trees in shafts. The trees shot up behind the Redeemer like pillars. The morning smelled of dew and horse piss (not much else, since the Messessagey hadn't camped there long enough to make their usual mess). Everything was growing, shooting, smelling, boiling with life, and I was remembering how much I loved my life with the Messessagey. The Redeemer remained silent. Perhaps he knew the tumult of the moment for me. I think he did. Even now.

Finally, I made signs that I would collect my things and mount behind him. I said, "So, ye finally come to save me from the heathen savages."

The Redeemer said, "If there was any decent heathen savages left, I'd leave you to them. But they ain't. The good ones all went west. The ones we got left can't live without white people."

"Then why're you here?" I said.

"I forget," he said. "I have a white wolf, a blazing sun, inside my skull. It makes me forget."

I had not set a-horse for a million years, and I could feel the Redeemer catch his breath when I grabbed his shoulders. The baby rode between us a-sucking on the Redeemer's coat. Red Dog went down the trail ahead of us. Scattering Light's head jounced against my thigh.

I looked around. Maybe Approaching Thunder was watching from the underbrush. Maybe some of my people were weeping on the trail as they moved away toward the west. I wasn't weeping. My heart was torn in two long before this. I thought, Oh shit, now I am going to have to learn to be white again.

(Now the Redeemer was dying. Night and day, he was dying.)

Priapism and Violent Memories

I have a visitor.

His other name is Head-Piercer, and he is my brother.

He wears a black beaver hat with a turkey vulture feather but otherwise looks much as he did when he caressed Boyd at Little Beard's Town on the Genesee. His face is painted black. After we greet each other, he takes out his instruments and, with calm deliberation, begins to operate.

Woe! Woe! they sing.

Hearken ye!

This is how it ends. I see the four of them—the boy, the girl, the old man racked with pain, and his black-haired lover. The old man is me. We camp beside a river, which looks familiar but is not the river we once knew. An imitation river. They call this place Canada, and it is mainly good for growing fur animals and rocks. It is an imitation country, a land of shadows. Once I thought I was the new Adam of this place, but already my seed was sickly and so could not start a fresh line.

There are Indians about. Mohawk, Oneida, Cayuga, Onondaga, and Seneca. The same Indians who were our neighbors where we once lived. Everyone drifting west from the Niagara, looking to escape the war. And some Messessageys who are the real owners of the place. "Grandfather, come and live with us," the Messessagey said. "Come and dwell among us and be happy. The war cannot touch you." They are just as confused as we are.

It is as if only now we are awakening from a five-year sleep and do not precisely recollect where we have been. Thinking to find ourselves at home we peer about for old familiar things. But this is not our home. It is an imitation home.

Was that the dream or is this the dream?

Woe! Woe! the singers sing.

Up and down the new river, *Woe! Woe!*

I have the headaches yet.

The pain begins behind my right eye, radiates across my jaw to my ear, snakes up and fills the vein that stands out on my forehead. When the pain reaches my forehead my face is suddenly split in two. The right side is on fire, and the left is in shadow.

Only they are worse.

Dr. McCausland recommends eye drops and a tonic and advises me to refrain from alcohol. Then he adds, "But it won't do you any good. The brain has begun to disintegrate."

Hearken ye!

We are diminished!

When the headache comes, I bid them tie me to a ladder-back chair and bind boiled apple halves over my eyes, and I set there a-shouting in the dark, clasping in my hand a little mask fetish (the image of my pain), which my wife has given me. The savages have a remedy—muskrat root, which we call water hemlock. She Walks the Sky calls it "husband killer." She keeps my guns locked up.

Woe! Woe!
The cleared land has become a thicket.
Woe! Woe!
The clear places are deserted.
Woe!

I remember the reason for Alice Kissane's anger when I marched out that spring—she wished not to be left but to come on the warpath with me (it is the Iroquois custom for women to join a war party from time to time, to fight or for pillage). She followed me to Oswego on the boat from Niagara with the Rangers and their supplies, and we took turns riding Miehlke along the river path (my mare was much used up with hard campaigning, and I thought we'd eat her before the snow flew). When I walked, my feet slipped in blood inside my boots.

Alice was pleased to see me. When she came off the boat, she kissed me and wrapped her hair around my neck so that I might not pull away or protest. She lifted her skirt and rubbed herself against my trouser front till the dampness seeped through. (Once I made her blush, saying her thing looked like a little squirrel had crept up and gone to sleep between her thighs—she herself in bawdy moments called it Mister Fuzzy.) Her silver brooches cut into my chest, she was so fierce.

But presently we saw a soldier mocking us, and I kicked him in the crotch and took her away with me.

Hearken ye!
We are diminished!

Disintegrate! I believe that is the word he used (I also suffer from priapism—a constant, embarrassing erection—and violent memories). If disintegration is my disease, then I caught it from the

world. Everything splits, or doubles, and splits or doubles again
and again, then whirls and whirls. I am at the heart of the whirlwind, the moment of storm. It is unnerving and unnatural.

This pseudohome, this mock river—they are something like
a place I once knew. What we have is a clearing my two slaves
have hewn out of the wilderness and a grid of white-maple stakes
in the ground where I intend to build a house as grand as Sir
William's. Oskar burned the real one, but has apologized. Though
I mistrust his apologies—he is very civil, very white, you might
say, but I believe he harbors ill feelings because I kept him from
being ordinary, because I saved him from mere reason and from
history. (I loved you, boy. My methods may have been wrong,
but I never stopped loving you. Was it sinful of me to try to save
you from yourself?)

If I am sick of anything, it is failure. I'm sick of failing all
the tests of life. The failure quotient is very high today, especially
as I have to sit and live my life in this imitation world, writing
my begging, whining, charming letters to the simpletons at Fort
Niagara and Quebec or the Board of Trade in London, while
Scotch traders, English half-pay officers, and New Jersey fence-
jumpers-turned-King's-men strut around like imitation founders,
bluestockings, and aristocrats—because that is what failures end
up doing. So here I am upset, self-hating, failed, mad, trapped, in
darkness (with my brain disintegrating)—all the indications and
motions are negative today. I wish I could find a pinch of that
husband killer or some other kind of rat poison.

Oskar—my son, the letter writer—came today during one of my
tranquil moments (I was passing time catching flies with the tip
of my tongue). I only half felt like a-killing him with my table
knife. When my hand reached out to take his throat, it suddenly
bethought itself and flicked a nubbin of lint off his collar instead.
At the same time, I smelled the reek of genever upon his breath.

I expressed sundry welcoming sentiments, the fine phrases
only somewhat marred by my new habit of inserting the word

"betrayal" at the pauses. (This country, by which I mean the people round about, Indian and white, has been betrayed once, twice, a hundred times. The land stinks of betrayal, condescension, and Englishmen.) He affected not to notice. Strangely, I had the impression his face was painted black, and he wore a turkey vulture feather in his hair.

He said She Walks the Sky had sent for him, that I was dying. This was news to me, I told him. Aside from a little disintegration, I never felt better. He said the Americans field a better army this year than last, that they built sixty-three new strong points between Schenectady and German Flatts, with flying columns of militia and Continentals ready for the alarum. In October, Colonel Willet came on so fast he brought Oskar's column to bay in the snowy woods at Johnstown, where Oskar got his wound, then came on again like a terrier after the first repulse and killed young Walter Butler in the rear guard at West Canada Creek.

(I weep for the lost sons of friends.)

Oskar complained endlessly of his wound, which he said might still prove fatal (though he looked lively enough to me). He walked with a splint on his leg and a stick under his arm. His hair was shaved except for a scalp lock. His face was scarred and charred from musket sparks, and his hands shook uncontrollably. He wore white men's clothes and a scarf done up around his neck to hide his tattoos (he is already ashamed of the thing that is most important about him).

He had seen the white girl the Messessagey call the One Who Remembers. She is the last one I shall ever redeem. I don't have the stomach for it and would not have bothered had not Wabecamegot and Approaching Thunder come a-begging me to take her off their hands. To their minds, she had become a witch much too powerful to abide. (Oncet I went to her myself. She made me drink a tonic she mixed from the dried inner bark of bur oak, red oak, and aspen, the root, bud, and blossom of the balsam poplar, and a small amount of snakeroot. She mixed the medicines in the kettle, adding them from the east side a little at

a time and muttering the magic word wabunong, eastward. I believe it did me some good.)

For a boy so recently wounded, suffering from loss of blood,
fever, not to mention delirium and murderous impulses toward
his relatives, Oskar's interest in the girl was uncommon hot. I
suddenly recognized something of myself in him. But I forbore
from answering on account of a headache coming on.

My Father Was Wrong
(from Oskar's Book about Indians)

My father was wrong to think I could not be redeemed, that the
words did not redeem me, that the dreams would stop. There
came a time when everyone else was dead, but their words lived
on in my book. The book remained like the shadows of dead
Indians, playing its little jokes upon the living.

There came a time when, all at once, I thought to myself, I
am the book. I am the one who tells the story. I am the One
Who Remembers and the Redeemer, the boy Oskar, and General
George. I wield the death maul, don the mask of another, and
dance the dance, shooting arrows at the sun. My words are arrows. They fall short.

Old Berbel Klock used to tell stories about wermen and wer-
women, creatures who changed into animal shapes on certain
nights of the year and went forth to do battle with demons and
witches who promised to interfere with the crops or turn the wine
sour. Then the Christians came and turned the people against
their own protectors, these nighttime shape changers. The wermen, half man, half wolf, became the enemy of the Roman
Church, and slowly they were stamped out (with the rack and
the iron maiden and red-hot pincers to the testicles). The One

Who Remembers told me about bear walking, about savages who had the ability to change themselves into animals and roam through the forest emitting flames and smoke from their mouths. Of course, I was struck by the strange congruence of beliefs, white and savage. (I dreamed the dreams Mary Hunsacker dreamed— we were all in some inflated state of mental activity, the result of war and the sudden mixing of languages.)

Despite everything, I think my father was a godly man, smitten with divinity; while George Washington broke himself and his honor on the altar of reason. I do not believe in God (old Europe, the King, loyalty, and authority) or reason (Locke's blank slate, history, atoms, laws, freedom, and democracy). To think that men can govern themselves is as idiotic as thinking they will forever bend the knee to someone better. Men and women are always being better or worse than you expect them to be. Their habit is to surprise you. Their lives are a mystery. (Even my own is a mystery to me, after all this writing.)

I remember Sundays when my mother lay dying, and I would join Sophronia and Toby Catchpole in the family pew in the Palatine Church. The limestone church had a balcony, a spiral pulpit, a sounding board, and a spire paid for by the Nellis clan. Atop the spire perched a weather vane with a bronze rooster. (The image of the weather vane reminds me of the night of my capture. In Colonel Bolton's records, it is written that Hendrick "recovered" his son from the Rebels; but my father always used the biblical word "redeemed.")

Catchpole whistles through his nose during the sermon and shouts, "Amen. Ama-a-a-a-ayn!" from time to time, though he cannot understand Dominie Frederici's German. This makes the Negroes who stand at the back of the church under the balcony shuffle their bare feet and snicker and disrupts the service, though the Germans only grumble about the Negroes. Sophronia snuggles so close to Catchpole she is practically in his lap. And they hold hands while pretending to read the hymnal, though neither one of them has letters.

In the late afternoon, we ride three astride on the long-suffering Army to my grandfather Georg Klock's fortified house in St. Johnsville to eat mounds of turkey, pork, squash, potatoes, and crab apples with my mother's brothers, sisters, aunts, uncles, and cousins. Old Berbel Klock, the matriarch, sits at the head of the table passing wind and sneezing on the food, which she cuts into pieces and feeds by hand to her favorite grandchildren, who come to her like dogs when called.

Berbel suffers from some disease or curse which is slowly turning her skin to leather, curling her hands up like wooden claws, and causing her mouth to grow to a small, pouty hole. She looks exactly like one of Tom Wopat's Whistler masks. She swears the dwarf Witcacy is a wizard who can dry up cows, make lovers impotent, or turn children into monsters in the womb. She blames him for teaching my father to read and scribe, thus turning him away from his kin onto the path of obstinate loyalty. (Though the truth is Witcacy did not mix in politics and only criticized the German settlers for a certain narrowness of outlook and inability to read and for preferring to pile their manure on the river ice in winter rather than spread it on the land.)

Berbel crosses her fingers and mutters spells when his name is mentioned. She wears a necklace of garlic. She paints a cross on her door and calls on Dabold Tum, the letter writer, to print the names of the saints along the arms and upright of the cross. In her mind, she and Witcacy were having a war of spells.

Witcacy, reading his books and sawing his fiddle bow, was never aware of the thunderbolts and maledictions crashing round his head.

When I think of it now, it makes me laugh.

Chanters of the Dead

Oskar is a creature of night, catnaps during the day, and hugs his guns or his pen close in the darkness. Nights, his leg seems to grow worse; he thinks of death, breaks into cold sweats, watches his own limbs being cut off one by one and carried off on platters. (At the Ranger hospital, he watched McCausland operate a dozen times, flinging arms and legs about like cordwood. The worst was when the doctor probed a fresh stump with his curved tenaculum, hooking out severed veins and arteries, which writhed like snakes, spurting blood till they died hissing against the red-hot cauterizing iron.)

Out upon the river flats, he hears the low susurration of the savage chants, the thudding of the water drums, the clacking of the turtle rattles, the rhythmic hymn of despair. Up and down the river, they are singing.

The cleared land has become a thicket.

The clear places are deserted.

And beyond that he hears the hammering of hammers on nails and the shouts of children and the lowing of cattle. The plow strikes a stone; the great tree falls with a roar that shivers the earth.

A charred log drops in the grate. Coals skitter across the hearthstones. A red dog, sleeping before the fire, whimpers in its sleep.

Woe! Woe! they sing.

Hiss, hiss, go the veins against the iron.

(Some of this is in the future.)

Presently, Oskar smells the smell of burning dog. He throws a dried apple at the dog's head. The dog lurches to its feet, circles five times, and drops again on the blackened stone. A child cries out in its sleep in the next room. Oskar hears the soft sh-sh sound of a woman's voice comforting the baby, lulling it back to sleep. Oskar wishes she would not speak to the child in Indian.

Then she begins to sing. It is a lullaby. The words are German, something she remembers from her own childhood. He remembers the words and tune himself because Margrethe used to sing it to him. In the next room, the woman begins to weep. Why she weeps is a mystery. Her name is the One Who Remembers.

On the table in front of him—a pair of green-glass spectacles and a red and black mask, sopping with goose grease. The mask gleams up at him.

Hearken ye!

We are diminished!

He writes: "The Dog is more Trouble than he is worth. He run off Today for an Hour & Mary thought he was dead. The Dog is from her former Lover, the one who lost his Face at Klock's Field, the day Tom Wopat died."

In the morning, he caught the One Who Remembers speaking to George Cunningham, his father's carpenter, who can neither read nor write. George is a reckless youth, swings himself among the rafter beams like an ape, sings Irish ballads for his dinner, and carves her little animal figurines from pine slivers. Oskar stutters when he speaks to her, sometimes cannot speak.

When she changes his dressings, she traces the blue-black tattoos on his skin with her fingers, explores the dimpled scars of his many wounds, murmuring savage incantations, praying, he thinks.

His father said, "I am dying, child." And the way he said it made Oskar sob.

Sleepless, he wraps himself in a buffalo robe by the fire (the red dog now asleep at his feet) and writes: "Dear Gen'l Washington, on Sunday fortnight by Joseph Brant's Boy Isaac I rec'd Word my Father, yer Olde Enemie, was a-dying at his Post at Little York in Canada among the Messessagey. The Message was for me to leave the Ranger Hospital at all Cost & ride hard to him for a Blessing. (My Horse army was down with Spavin. I had to take a Nag & fell off the first Morning & would have died then except an Indian found me & brought me along.) I found my Father Moribund but Bad-Tempered as allway & stretched not upon his Death Bed but tied to a Chair & creating a Racket. At other times, he is lucid & dictates his will.

"This is what I think—The War has taught me a Grammar of Love. We—Rebels & Tories & Whites & Indians—are having a violent Debate whose Subject is the Human Heart, its constituent Elements & Humors, its hidden Paths. This is a Mystery. The Effect of the Argument, the Structure of its Thought, is a curious Splitting or Splintering. (I don't know if I think this or it is thinking me—this is the Way my Father would talk.)

"My Father tells me there is an ancient Iroquois Ceremony called the Ogiwe, the Big Kettle, wch is a Feast for ye Dead. He said We are but Singers of the great Dead, that we are Shadows addressing Shadows, that we only have our Memories & these are fading.

"As his brain disintegrates, sometimes my Father is an Indian, is a Woman, is a Child.

"When he saw me this afternoon, he shouted in Terror."

At night she tells him stories. She tells him about Nzagima and the Thunderers. She tells him about Nanebojo and his marvelous asshole. She tells him about Approaching Thunder and Wabanooqua and Scattering Light, about Annonk, or Star, and the Windigo. She tells him of the perfidiousness of plants and rocks. She recites tales with strange names like "How the One Who Remembers Fought the Toad." Most arresting of all is the terrible story of her own capture:

There was no one. Then they were there.

They were silent as sunlight.

She tells Oskar stories till he falls asleep from pure exhaustion, and, when he sleeps, he dreams. In his dreams, he sees the headless corpse (she carries the head of her lover in a bag—it makes him gag to think about it). In another part of the unfinished house, his father shrieks (the rope-mesh bedsprings go creak-creak and Alice Kissane moans). Oskar tries to curl up closer to the One Who Remembers, but she lies patiently till she thinks he is asleep again, then moves away.

In Pennsylvania that spring, he led ten white men and thirty savages on a raid. He was a wraith, a war ghost, a thin shadow, dusted with gunpowder and dandruff. The porcupine quills in his hair clicked when he walked, and the bare skin around his scalp lock glistened red from paint and sweat. He spoke Indian, even to the whites. He wore the green-glass spectacles and carried a tattered umbrella into battle. At midwinter, he had fasted and chopped a mask from a basswood tree, an ugly face with brass eyelets and a crooked nose and mouth grinning in glee and agony. He carried the mask in a bag. Sometimes, he danced the dance and sang the song Tom Wopat had taught him. The only time he was warm was when the sun shone full and hot at midday. Otherwise, his teeth rattled with chills. Joseph Brant said boiled rattlesnake would cure the ague. Oskar had slaughtered rattlesnakes by the hundreds. He lived on snake. He tied the rattlers round his wrists and ankles. He painted his face, half-red, half-black.

He and his men went openly, courting battle. Others might grumble against the tactic, but Oskar said he would shoot skulkers in the balls. He was still incompetent but scary. Even the Indians didn't understand how he stayed alive.

They herded cattle and horses into barns and burned the barns. They cut off wood gatherers and left them pinned to the trees with their axes. They were in the business of making widows. Oskar's white men dressed as Indians; the Indians dusted their faces with wheat flour to make themselves look white and covered their tattoos and feathers with homespun shirts, cast-off suits, and beaver hats.

Once, three miles from Frankstown in Bedford County, a company of militia stood up to them in a thicket. Oskar and his men were jog trotting between devastations, eating pork (or maybe roast hired man) from the last barn fire but one. They extended their line on either side without breaking stride, Oskar with a heavy brass blunderbuss pistol in either hand and a knife between his teeth.

The Pennsylvanians fired a ragged volley, which went high on account of terror and black-powder recoil, and gave themselves up for lost. "Quarter! Quarter!" they cried out quaintly, in the old-fashioned way, mostly addressing Indians whom they took for white men. The Indians shouted "Quarter!" back and shot a few, letting the rest escape.

They had a glut of scalps. They were sated with hair.

Oskar counted one of his own men dead and two wounded. The Rebels lost thirteen dead, seven wounded, and five taken prisoner.

An old man who couldn't run on account of a gamy leg sat on a stump and wept. He said he had two sons among the corpses. Oskar ordered the bodies brought and propped up at the old man's feet.

"Here," he said. "Ye kin have them back. Tell them we ain't savages."

The old man snarled, "Not them two! Those other'n over there."

So they shot him.

When he does nod off (which is rare), Oskar dreams of ships foundering, armies marching, of a masked boy dancing and shooting arrows at the sun. Once he dreamed of a white woman with her hair off, crawling over wagon ruts and moaning. And once he shot a sow bear that, dying, became a naked girl more beautiful than any female he had ever seen.

From talking to Mary, he knows he is dreaming the dreams

of others, that the dreams are migrating, that he is losing his own dreams as they are slowly replaced by someone else's.

The headless tattooed man is the worst. When he dreams of his friend Tom Wopat, his dream-self becomes obsessed with unraveling the mystery of the blue designs. He reads and he reads, but remembers nothing when he wakes up.

The woman is known as the One Who Remembers. Her real name is Mary Hunsacker. They call the baby Dumpling, but her real name is Aurora, which is the dawn. She is named for an old Messessagey wabeno witch. For the Messessagey, east is the direction of the current of life. It makes Oskar uncomfortable to think about.

Woe! Woe! they sing.
Hearken ye!
We are diminished!

Oskar Will Get This Part Wrong

Oskar will get this part wrong, so I must tell it myself.

The first time I saw him he looked terrified, stern, willful, pale, dirty, angry, proud, disappointed, confused, uncertain, righteous, stubborn, shy, curious, and familiar (he had Scattering Light's look). He was sore wounded in the leg below the knee and used a stick to walk with. I knew then how everything would turn out. I knew already I would die and he would die (but before that, he would wander off and marry a real white woman) and that one day he would give my girl the book about Indians and tell her the story of us. I knew this, as if somewhere, in another book, it was already written.

Under his clothes, Oskar was half-Indian. Except when he was writing things down (he collected facts like butterflies, pinning them to the pages, dead), he was melancholy, wishing he had been a dashing American instead of an unwilling Tory. He had a soft spot for widders and fat girls and, like his father, women who had done it with Indian men. He had an affinity for the edges of civilization—people at the edge are always closer to the other, more tolerant of difference; this tolerance brands them as sinful; it is a brand and a badge.

We recognized each other from our dreams. We had courted each other in our dreams. (Oskar wallowed in a stream of dreams, which he wished he could dam up.)

At first he was sicker than he thought (then again, he thought he was a-dying, and he weren't that sick). A Messessagey hunter found him limping upon the trail, looking for his horse, uttering a fevered jumble of words, curses, and maledictions, his wound festering and turning black. When he saw the hunter, he threw himself on the man's neck, sighing, "Tom. Tom." He slept a night and a day and woke up demanding gin and paper.

I brought him soup in a pan and fixed gunpowder toddies. I put maggots to eat the putrid flesh, then scraped and rewrapped his wound and felt to make sure the leg was setting properly. I applied poultices and irrigations and sang my song the way Wabanooqua had taught me.

Oukaquiqua nipoumin, quiticog manido-o-o.

These were the first kind things a body had done for Oskar, possibly in his whole life, and I believe it caused him to fall in love at once, like a stone, though, at times, in his delirium, he addressed me as Widder Tibbs, so I could not be sure.

Also he recognized the song.

The gods say that we shall die one day.

The gods say. . . .

I did not fall in love. I had a sick feeling that if I loved Oskar, he would die (like you know who).

Oukaquiqua nipoumin, quiticog manido-o-o.

("I know those words," Oskar said, and fell in love.)

*   *   *

I was nervous, having forgot how to talk to a white boy. Wubbo Ockels was my onliest previous experience, and, now that I think on it, we did not speak. When he was able, I took Oskar down to the river and pointed out the island place where his father wished to be buried. I asked him would he dance the dance for me. I asked him did he know any more songs. I asked him how it felt to kill a man. I asked what war was like and if it were a good way to meet women. (He said yes.)

He had so many old wounds, so many lumps on his head, an elbow that failed to bend, patches of burnt or discolored skin, a little finger missing from his left hand, and that dirty bandage and splint with his boot slit open and tied round the splint. He was a roving field hospital, an education in surgery, an experiment in what you can do to a human being and not kill him. The Messessagey respected him for it, though. They looked away when he walked by, the way they did when a person of power came on the scene. They didn't stare or inquire. They just knew he had walked at the edge of the world and looked out.

When I wouldn't let him kiss me, he wanted to know the names of my lovers (the number abashed him, and he limped off in a sulk). He asked to see Scattering Light's head, was sick, then came back and watched it for an hour, thinking. He kicked the dog around the house with his wounded leg, shouting every time.

His hair was stiff and bristly where it was growing in around his scalp lock. His leg wound stank. (It is true, though, that I put a love potion on it by mistake.) He followed the Nottaway custom and blabbed about his dreams, which at first was repugnant to me and made me frightened. Every time he opened his mouth he offended the Grandfathers. It was nothing like being with Scattering Light—the flute, the dog chasing the stick, and Approaching Thunder's strange dream. (Hopefully, I asked him did he play a musical instrument. No.)

When I spoke to Oskar, he was only half there. I would come upon him hunched over a table in an unfinished room, George Cunningham hand winching a log up a ramp behind him, Oskar scribbling on bark or scraps of paper or reading a book. Oncet I snuck up on him, and when I touched him, he fainted from fright. I believe also he was drunk a good deal of the time, which might explain his absentmindedness.

All the while, the Redeemer was a-dying. Days, I sat with him for solace—his or mine, it was difficult to tell. He bled himself, placed leeches upon his nose and watched them feed, or nicked his arms and legs. Dr. McCausland came every week or so and applied clysters, poultices, and flaming cups. He injected antimony and mercury, enough for a horse, and force-fed pills made of chalky clay and laudanum. When the headaches came, we tied the Redeemer to a chair to keep him from doing away with himself.

They said he was mad, but he made uncommon sense to me. He spoke Messessagey in preference to any other tongue. He had a voice like Approaching Thunder's. He called himself Split Face, Son of the Thunderer. He said he remembered me in the church with the bronze cock when I was small. He said it didn't matter if he went west (which was assuredly where he was a-going—the Head-Piercer had been augering into his skull for some time now—yes, yes, we had a certain pain and experience in common). He said what is important is to grapple with the other. He said the other is always a man or a woman, an Indian, a child, someone who speaks another language—that we are all darkened rooms to one another. He said violence has its own strange and perverse beauty—at least it makes you pay attention. You get to know a man when you're a-killing him, or when he's a-killing you.

The hardest for me was when Oskar tried to speak with his father, his face turning red, his voice hoarse and whispery. Sometimes he would only choke out the one word, "Why?" Afterward, I would lead him away and comfort him.

I already knew he would leave me.

I also knew that George Cunningham would die, squished under a barn wall he was a-putting up drunk, after giving me two more children to feed.

And oncet I woke from a dream and told Approaching

Thunder, "Make war on books. Die fighting. Don't live another day, another minute—it's only going to get worse."

Listen, I could tell you the future of all of us. But no one believes a prophet. So don't ask.

This is what I think: We have all bungled saving one another. We are all victims of botched attempts at salvation.

Hearken ye!

This is what I think: Even after I was saved, I wanted to be saved.

An Address to Pilgrims

I recall mostly, when I recall anything at all—on account of my disintegrating brain, I have total recall of about five things, though at the moment I forget which five—the deaths of friends. (Perhaps they are only friends because they are dead—the dead have a certain probity, a certain moral heft, which I find wanting amongst those who are still walking around alive.)

Mason Bolton drowned sailing into retirement on his schooner, the *Ontario*, an eighteen-gunner with a shallow hull, which the shipwrights had warned him of. Young Walter Butler died in a fresh linen shirt with a lace cravat and paisley waistcoat while saluting Colonel Willet's attacking force, which nevertheless took advantage of his stationary moment to shoot him through the chest. (Life was all theater to him, that was the way he got through things, but I don't think for a moment he ever saw people for what they were.)

Tageheunto disappeared in a raid on a Kentucky settlement along the Scioto. A man's flayed body was found sometime later with his head thrown back and his mouth gaping in an expression of rage or agony or astonishment. It was thought to be his on no evidence except that it was a body. And no one had time to bury it.

Tom Wopat died at the Noses. It scarcely bears mentioning.

Tell me, does it rob my story of its mystery to know that we all die?

I have a visitor. His other name is Head-Piercer, and he is my brother.

Margrethe had a yellow dog. Something reminded me of that today. Seeing her play with it made me love her. The fake river here is called by the Messessagey the Pesshinneguning Oeshino, or the One That Washes the Timber Down and Drives Away the Grass Weeds, which about sums it up. It is shallow and muddy, and I miss the great mountains rolling up on either side of the valley.

If I could sit a horse, I'd be gone in a minute. It galls me, not having killed enough Americans yet (not that I really have anything against Americans—it is just that they are handy and belligerent). What does it mean to live in a nation that finds its identity in its losses and twists them into victories? In public, Oskar already wears a wig and denies that he once shaved his head save for a scalp lock and painted his face red and black with a line down the middle. One day he will deny it so often that he will forget it. And then how will he know who he is or how he came to be?

Woe! Woe!

The cleared land has become a thicket.

The clear places are deserted.

I saw a naked child scoot by me on her hands and knees the other day, chasing a red dog from room to room. She had a face that reminded me of Oskar when I dandled him on my knee and made his corn-husk dolly speak in Mohawk till he laughed. It made me wistful to see.

This is how it ends—with me going under the ground somewhere I do not recognize and the savage chanters intoning my dirge and the ashy-faced chiefs counting off the names on their condoling canes.

Woe! Woe! they sing.

We are diminished!

Oskar scribbles down everything I say and then makes queer little remarks which remind me how alien and prosaic he seems. I say, The grave is a mouth gaping open before me. I say, I sometimes believe I am an Indian called Split Face. I say, Boy, I have lost everything. Oskar says yes (and makes a note).

Though I remember well the day he led his warriors shrieking into the fog of death by the Noses. For a moment then, I thought he had possibilities.

My father (now dead) came indentured to slave in the tar camps on the Livingston Patent in the Hudson Valley. He was a pitch boiler in the forest, living in a hut. This made him hate the English. In 1711, he went for a soldier with Governor Nicholson's army against the French, an expedition which came to naught. Then he crossed the Helderbergs with his brother to the Schoharie and bought land of the Mohawk. But the Dutch merchants at Orange had a prior title and threw him off. With George Klock he schemed against the Indians and got their land. I believe he had no choice in the matter, but it went hard with the savages.

Oddly, since the boy is about, I think more of my father. Perhaps it is only that I see in Oskar my own hatred and rebellion, and when I see it I am taken aback. I recognize his face; it is a mask of my own. I think, What if my father was as doubtful and prone to error as I am myself? It makes me sweat to entertain such thoughts. At every step I misdoubted myself. I used to beat the boy on account of it, to dissemble my confusion. I hoped he would understand, that words of humiliation need not pass between us, that he would forgive me.

The war made everything strange.

I think of my father who lost two countries before he was

sixteen, two homes, one with a vineyard attached and a view of the Rhine, the other a tent on a heath at the edge of London. (Once he told me about a Gypsy girl there who let him rive her in a ditch. It haunted him, he said. When he came to New York, he saw a dozen like her in every Indian town.)

This is what I think: Behind the mask, there is only another mask.

My brain is disintegrating. That's Dr. McCausland's considered medical opinion.

Woe! Woe!

There is a girl about the place who has a silver plate in her skull (in the shape of a mask). She has a bear-paw bag with a man's head in it. I have tripped over her dog a dozen times that I can recall. She hates tulip trees and is a terrible cook. Now that she is safely my responsibility the Messessageys come around to visit her at all hours and often spend the night in my broad central hallway (unroofed as yet). She makes them laugh and leads them in songs and reminds them of things they have forgotten. She brews up native medicines in my kitchen where Queenie, the Negro wench, is teaching her spells and potions from her own people along the River Niger in Africa. The place smells a fright, but she is kind to me.

If it weren't for the Indians, I'd have no place, since the English are uncommon slow at admitting they have lost the war and my land and making restitution. "Grandfather, come and live with us," the Messessagey begged. (The Iroquois were already setting up shop in the valley of the Messessagey, white folk marching up the lakeshore.)

How nervous, strident, and ill humored it makes us, pretending to the old order and eyeing the birth pangs of the grand republic to the south. (Fresh news from the nonwar: Cornwallis surrenders at Yorktown. Tell me, if there is a God, why did He give the Rebels all the generals?)

Woe! Woe! they sing.

Disorder, disintegration, and betrayal—these are the words that come to mind when I am in agony. Odd that the word "disintegration" accompanies the very process of disintegration in my brain. Odder still, I seem, on the whole, to be losing my English speech when the Indian words remain vivid and accessible. Once I said that becoming an Indian was like unto entering a swarming madness, but it might redeem you. I mean going out of yourself, abandoning the structure of mind which is peculiarly white, entering that area where, because it is neither one nor the other, you are nothing.

It is a strange adventure. But aside from the pain and my constant irritability (which is unpleasant for the ones I love), I am not unwilling to attempt it.

What I say is, We are all pilgrims, Pilgrim.

We are on a journey, I know not whence nor where.

Love difference.

Lo! I have a visitor.

His face is painted black.

Field of Bones
(from Oskar's Book about Indians)

History is a field of bones.

My father said that briefly during the war, betwixt the English and the Americans, we had a grand republic of races and languages, a flame, he said, of true freedom (and anger), or just a glimmer, between the King and the universality of reason. He said reason would make slaves of everyone, but he'd be dead by then, ha ha. I fear this existed mostly in his mind and is now forgot (though my graffiti skin bears witness to it).

A restless wind blows vacantly through the land now, driving us to parsimony and regret. My neighbors are all of a conservative and commercial bent with not a gambler or a risk taker among them. Thin piety is the state religion. And they have acquired a pernicious snobbery from the English half-pay officers and remittance men who come here to be gentlemen on the cheap. My wife is one such colonial blue blood, but she was redeemed (intermittently) by her sensual appetites, which were marked and peculiar. In bed, my scars and tattoos excited her, though otherwise in public she pretended they did not exist. This doubleness redeemed her.

Once, after the war, I rode south, crossed the Niagara River, and got as far as Conesus, where the Negro war chief Captain Sun Fish had built his village. Americans were living in the Indian houses, digging up corn caches, grazing cattle and pigs in the peach orchards. I said I was from Virginia and had fought with a regiment of the line under General Greene. I paid for a bed and stayed three days, afraid to go outside. One night a simple girl, sent by the tavern owner, let me touch her privates. In the morning, I rode away, back to Canada, certain I would never fit anywhere.

Which was true.

Yesternight, I dreamt a dream. An ancient woman came to me. She had a strange shambling walk. Her feet were shod in moccasins in the shape of bear paws, with huge claws that clicked and scratched as she walked. She lifted her doeskin smock and let me see her scraggy nether hair and the tattoos that covered her body. The tattoos glowed in the dark. I ran my fingers over them, tracing the familiar designs. She pointed at the sky, and I saw, quite suddenly, the patterns of her body repeated point for point in the night sky. She was Ji-gon-sa-seh, Mother of Nations, Mother of the World. (My father, too, had dreamed of her.)

This was a dream of death.

Oskar Limps down to the River to Die

The unfinished hallway, the storerooms, the trading room, even the privies, are crowded with guests and mourners. Oskar can no longer find a place to sleep. Mary has moved to a wigwam in the dooryard. Her bed beneath the canvas has been taken by an Indian family, a Mr. and Mrs. Thunder. Toby Catchpole leads the Christians in morning and evening prayers. Sophronia, blowsy in her first pregnancy, weeps and blows her nose on an old letter (Oskar shudders to think it might be one of his own letters misdelivered).

Mary's daughter runs wild with the Indian children. When Oskar sees Dumpling, he can barely distinguish the child from his memories, she reminds him so much of himself in some other life. He half expects to see Tom Wopat round the corner, resplendent in his new green-glass spectacles.

His father shouts. Some terrible delirium has gripped his mind, some evil memory come to torture him at the last. (Attending to him is difficult on account of the leeches hanging from his cheeks, not to mention the smell and his constant rampant state, which makes a mockery of his pain.) Dr. McCausland shakes his head and knocks back another glass of whiskey. The shouts and screams unnerve even him. He buries his nose in his Latin pharmacopoeia.

Tinkers, traders, and local ladies have set up shop on trestle tables in the yard and along the road, selling kettles and ax heads, apple pies and whiskey from puncheons. Someone's pet bear escapes every night and gets into the chicken coop or hog pen. Water drums and turtle rattles fill the night air. The chanters chant. It is mystery and a rebuke to Oskar that the Indians revere his father so.

Woe! Woe! they sing.

Hearken ye!
We are diminished!

Nightfall. Oskar paces before the fire, limping up and down upon his stick, dragging his foot. Insomnia is the name of the country he lives in. His nerves are in a permanent state of uproar. Like every other man and woman, white or Indian, in the new Tory settlements, Oskar remembers, is mired in remembering. His primary mode of thought is nostalgia, and what was bad seems good, and what was good seems better as long as it was before.

Dr. McCausland rouses from a nap upon the table bench, calls for another hot grog, and inquires if Oskar needs examining, if he can prescribe a little something, a tonic or stimulant or sleeping draft. Perhaps amputation is long overdue.

Oskar takes up a loaded pistol, his buffalo robe, his bag of papers, his mask, and Tom Wopat's green-glass spectacles and flees in a fog of pain to the solitude of the riverbank. He nests down among the roots of an ancient willow, takes out a nubbin of charcoal pencil, and writes by the moon. Oskar writes: "My Father is a-dying. This is a disappointment as I would have preferred to kill that snake myself."

He scratches an angry line beneath the words and writes again: "Enclosed *A Historie of the Recent Campaign, Cont'd*, Last Words scribed by a deceased Soldier of the Kinge, in his own Memory, & dedicated to General George Washington, a Man also embarrassed by a Tory Parent, namely, his Mother. My dear General,—an Addendum to my Previous—I cannot say how my present Condition grieves me. I wanted to be a General of the New Republic, too. I wanted to listen only to the Voice of Reason. I wanted to lead Men in the Cause of Liberty. I wanted to believe that Providence is benign, that History tends toward Perfection, that Men can govern their Impulses & Emotions & live together in Peace & Prosperity. But instead I became a Lord of Darkness, a Field Commander of Imps & Demons, Heir to

Division & Paradox, my Father's Estate, with wch he has been Kindly & Liberal (his Species of Kindliness being a Curse).

"These Letters are a long Letter I write & for the most Part do not send. My Body is the new Book & it is a Book of Suffering & Loss. The Words pour out of me onto the Sheet, the Image of my Melancholy. Is it true that I was once a happy Childe? Could it be that I was kidnapped & forced to War by Paternal Imperative? Have I slept with Widders & slaughtered my Friends? These tattoos of mine, got in a Drunken Stupor, tell a strange Tale, unbelievable even to me.

"There was a Woman in Dogtown below the Fort (where I got my Tattoos), Name of Beatrice Wimple, who made a Living all that Winter in back of a Tavern. She was hugely Obese & Melancholy & we sat together over many a Pot tho she did not recognize me from the Past, even mistook me for an Indian most times (despite that I occasionally tried to clean myself & dress in Clothes). Oh, how I once ached for her whom now I pity. When the cold Weather broke, she beat her Husband to Death with a lead Tankard, stole a cart Horse from the Livery, rode half-Naked to the Falls and threw herself in (the Falls are a favorite spot for young Lovers, Adulterers & Suicides, a Place of Fatal Attractions—sometimes the Bodies of Suicides or Drunks or doomed Lovers impeded shipping they were so Frequent).

"My Arme is weary, my Hearte is heavie, my Pen I droppe, never again to write a Word—

"Yrs. the late Oskar Nellis."

He writes: "P.S. Witcacy has the Gout & the Stone & his Skin is like brown Paper. He says I am a Natural Writer, that I suffer a characteristic Distemper, a Doubleness of Mind, & that the best Writing comes from Exile, Disease, Treason, Secrecy & Translation. He says it is Wrong to regard the Negroes & Savages, Peoples routed & enslaved, as Primitives with a greater Morality than our own. After dealing with the Perversity of Whites for so long, they are the most complicated, devious, corrupt, insane & advanced Beings on Earth. & they will have their Revenge in Two Hundred Years or so, when they finally convince us to doubt ourselves.

"Having writ this, I retire my Pen, may it ne'er speake again (it is snowing a little)."

He writes: "P.P.S. One word further—I have followed yer recent Career in the Papers & it is surely impolite & discourteous of me not to spare a Line for your own Misery. To wit, yer recent Humiliation when yer Mother went to the State House in Richmond for Support claiming you had abandoned her. What a Fish-wife she must be! May I never meet the like. My own Mother was an Embarrassment as well (seeing the Light & all) but not up to yer Mother's Mark & she died perforce before she did any serious Damage.

"I also hear Jackie Custis, yer worthless Step-Son went West at Yorktown (of Fever, of course, given his pusillanimous Temperment, not Battle Wounds). I am certain the goode Widder Custis, yer Wife, will not let you live it down. (Isn't it interesting that we have both had to do with Widders?)

"On that Note of Sympathy, I close my Memoirs."

He writes: "P.P.P.S. She won't let me. What promised to be a Glory of Love (for about a Week) is now a Husk. She laughs & cuddles the Child, & the Child laughs. At Night, she tells me Stories to pass the Time & prevent Intercourse.

"She claims to see the Future, & it irritates her. She says I'll find another Girl, one that shits in a Chamber Pot (& empties it outside in the Morning instead of just going outside in the first Place) & can read a Letter. She is Fiery & indignent despite my Denials. She says I already wear a Wig at the Fort to cover my Haircut. She says one Day they will say I have an Indian Childe & a Squaw (Forest Wife) & I will deny it.

"An Indian tried to sell me a Necklace of Chicken Bones

this Morning, saying they were the Bones of a White Moose w^ch
I could use to call Moose within Range of my Musket, or make
the Woman of my Dreams fall in Love with me, or see the Future.
I do not wish to see the Future or fall in Love. I wouldn't mind
being able to shoot a Deer now and then.

"Farewell, Oskar.

"The End.

"Finis.

"The Snow is letting Up & will melt in the Morning—"

Oskar nods off, his bare fingers turning blue upon the bark sheets.
He dreams the dream. He shoots the bear. The woman dies.

The sound of a footstep wakes him. At first he thinks it is
the captive bear escaped from its iron peg again and reaches for
his pistol. But the One Who Remembers appears out of the darkness, carrying Aurora in her arms.

She is like his mother, he thinks, easily impressed by writing
and by words. She has sat for hours, mesmerized by the flow of
ink across his pages, the scratching of the pencil point on paper,
the rhythmic undulations of the text she cannot understand.

The One Who Remembers says, "Stop thinking. Teach us
the dance. Teach the baby to sing."

"No," he says. "I can't anymore. My leg hain't whole—"

She touches his arm. She says, "I'll let you if you teach us'n."

He sighs and stands and slips off his shirt. His skin glimmers
like quicksilver in the moonlight and sifting snow. *He recalls going
down to the river, intending to do away with himself. The One Who
Remembers met him there. She said, Teach me the dance. Teach our
daughter the song.*

He hooks the green-glass spectacles over his ears and straps
the mask over his face. He tries a step or two, then stops. The leg
is sore but strong. But his legs feel awkward in trousers and doeskin gaiters. So he strips everything off and begins again, naked.

Oukaquiqua, he sings, *nipoumin, quiticog manido-o-o.*

Somewhere across the river a drummer drums. The drumbeat seems to get inside his chest. His ribs seem to vibrate with each blow. He feels immensely old and strong and sad.

Oukaquiqua, he sings, *nipoumin, quiticog manido-o-o.*

He sings in the Indian way, repeating the same words over and over. The words are a fever in the brain. Strange words and animal thoughts (dancing, he grows wings from his shoulders and paws for feet). The patterns imprinted upon his skin begin to glow and, glowing, repeat the patterns of the stars that show from time to time between the shreds of black cloud. This is what it is like to be a god, he thinks. You have only to think a thing and you become it.

Oukaquiqua, he sings, *nipoumin, quiticog manido-o-o.*

The gods say that we shall die one day.

The gods say . . .

Up the hill, his father shouts in his sleep. Alice Kissane murmurs in sympathy. Dumpling yawns and rubs her eyes. When she sees the mask, she shrieks with laughter. Oskar thinks, as though in a delirium: They have changed us. Stupidly, because of the scale of time, I have seen everything as timeless, complete. But they have changed us, just as surely as we are changing them. My father, Mary, Alice Kissane, all suffer a kind of lunacy, or what to white people looks like lunacy, and which is more a breach in their understanding which allows a new perspective. They are new things on the earth. Just as Tom Wopat entered a whirling madness going the other way, learning to be a white man. No longer white or Indian, what might we become?

He thinks: I have understood nothing. I don't even want to understand anything now. I want to stick to the truth. I decided long ago not to understand. If I try to understand anything, I shall mistake the truth.

Up and down the river, the chanters chant:

Woe! Woe!

Hearken ye!

We are diminished!

A Moment in the Wind

Hearken ye!

His other name is Head-Piercer, and he is my brother.

He wears a black beaver hat with a turkey vulture feather but otherwise looks much as he did when he caressed Boyd at Little Beard's Town on the Genesee. His face is painted black.

Woe! Woe! they sing.

Hearken ye!

I listen for a change in the weather that will be no weather. She Walks the Sky asks me my dreams, and I give them to her. I bequeath them to her. I have violent memories. Once I saw a woman crawling in the wagon ruts with her hair off, cursing. The most violent things are things that change your mind. He calls me Split Face.

Woe!

Dr. McCausland tells me I am disintegrating. This is a lie. I've never felt better. My head aches, though. My brain is a jangle of words and languages and prayers. I draw a knife down the centerline of my face and paint myself with blood. I saw a woman, moaning and cursing, crawling along a wagon rut. It did me good to see it.

Woe! Woe! they sing.

We are diminished!

The cleared land has become a thicket.

The clear places are deserted.

* * *

I am against the future. But I firmly believe that out of the collapse of everything something new arises. Crow is of some ancient race whose remnants live among the Iroquois—the Cat Nation, the Wenro, and the Neutral are some of their names. The last were sun worshipers, as I believe the Iroquois once were. (Down the Ohio, Oskar once saw huge earthen temple mounds and smaller mounds in the shapes of animals—birds, snakes, deer—which the local people did not recall erecting. These are mysterious remnants of lost civilizations which remind us only that we, too, shall die, that this frenzied dream of mankind—our great buildings, armies, kings, governments, and philosophies—will pass, that all is dust.)

I ask Crow had he ever met the one called Ji-gon-sa-seh, the Mother of Nations, or the Mother of the World. He says nothing, only throws the bones and reads my fortune and dances about me, singing and shouting, pretending to shoot me with invisible bullets from his bear-paw medicine bag. I recall, apropos of nothing, that when the Redcoats went in with the bayonet, amid their curses, they would shout, "Sliver them! Sliver the damned bitches!"

At length, the black savage takes his knife from the fire and begins to caress me about the balls. The pain is a white-hot worm of fire, a serpent of fire, that wiggles in my spine. I wriggle in my seat and spit screams. I am in a glory of pain. It is a bright and burning light.

(At this time, I am bound to the ladder-back chair overlooking the boat landing and the goose run and the hut where Alice Kissane lives with the girl I redeemed. There is a hog or a dog among the geese. Perhaps there is a rattlesnake down there. The hogs are well-known snake killers. They keep the vermin down along the river bottom and give tolerable company when you are alone. Heathen boys, stripped to their willies despite the cold, play a curious game in the cow meadow. I have seen them at it every day. Spectators come and go. But the game goes on. How I am able to see this with my eyes bandaged is a mystery.)

Between times, when I am mostly calm (tranquillity within the whirlwind is a sure sign of insanity), I compose my will: "I, Hendrick Nellis of Little York upon the Grand River in Canada, Yeoman, being throu' the abundant Mercy and Goodness of God, altho' in a decaying state of Health, yet of sound and perfect understanding and Memory, blessed be God, but calling to Mind the Mortality of my Body and knowing that it is appointed for all Men once to die . . ."

Tell me your dream, She Walks the Sky says, and I will cure you. But when I tell her, she throws her apron over her face and cries out. My visions are terminal. She is afraid I will drag her into the whirlwind.

Presently, Crow begins to work upon my fingers and toes. At first, I cannot tell what he is up to, my vision being restricted and all. He places glowing splinters beneath the nails where they sizzle and pop, the nails turning black and smoking. Then he wrenches out the nails so there is nothing left at the ends of my digits but smoking craters.

I ask him about the sun-worship side of things. He tells me about Agreskwe, the Great White Wolf, the Sun Wolf, the god of war and death, as he uses a stone knife to sever the knuckles of my fingers. Somewhere I am shouting and screaming. The women come running from their potato patch, their feet flinging off clods of muddy earth.

Crow kindles a fire at my feet, after which I begin to smell something cooking. He says it is good I am brave, that I do not whimper or cry out. He says usually they sacrifice a white dog nowadays, but he still prefers using an adopted enemy when he can get one. He places a necklace of red-hot ax heads round my neck. He says I am a glory to Agreskwe, a worthy opponent, a loud message for those in the Land of the Dead.

O Serpent of Fire, I think (apropos of nothing), wed me to my fate.

Crow slices holes in my skin, placing coals and burning brands within.

Hearken ye!

This is the Season of Fire, I think.

Hearken ye!

Let motion leave me, I think.

Hearken ye!

Let my bones rest upon the hillock yonder.

Hearken ye!

There is a moment in the wind when the wind stops.

Hearken ye!

The Whirlwind
(from Oskar's Book about Indians)

My wife says when I sleep now, I moan and grind my teeth, and my hand writes upon the pillow. What it writes she cannot say. And I do not tell her my dreams.

At night and at odd times during the day, I still hear Witcacy's peremptory summons, his call to battle. My blood gets up. My fingers begin to twitch and itch.

Are you ready? he shouts.

Are you ready to write?

Are you ready to tell the truth?

Yes.

Far away, a boy who is no longer a boy, aged before his time, chews the tip of his goose-quill pen to a mangle, sketches a star on the back of his hand, and takes a breath that is almost a sob, almost an exclamation of joy.

He writes: "I believe I am Lost & there is no Hope. I go to sleep at Night a-dreaming that I am Dying. When I am Dead, I sleep—

"tom Wopat made me wear a Mask. We a-danced in the Forest & sang the Song—'The gods say that we shall die one day. The gods say . . .'

"(Their Songs are werrie monotonous consisting as they do of the same Line repeated o'er and o'er. Also it was in some strange Tongue wch otherwise I did not recognize.)

"I danced & danced & presently perceived that I was Alone—still dancing.

"My Soul is become tainted with Savagery.

"In Life, we should not pretend lest We lose ourselves & become that wch we pretend to be.

"When you wear a Mask, you become the Mask.

"Tho I am haunted by my Father's Words, 'But it might redeem you.'

"Sometimes I dream there are only the Masks.

"I walk in a Forest of Trees carved with Masks, a Forest of Masks. Then a roaring, gibbering, whirling Wind comes & sweeps them away.

"I put these down as random Thoughts, in no particular Order, reflecting my State of Mind wch is now chaotic & un-formed as the Earth on the First Day."

A Note About the Author

Douglas Glover was born in Ontario, Canada, and now makes his home outside Saratoga Springs, New York, where he taught at nearby Skidmore College. Among his previous books, there are the short-story collection *A Guide to Animal Behavior* and the novel *The South Will Rise at Noon*.

He was recently writer-in-residence at the New York State Writers Institute.

A Note on the Type

The text of this book has been set in Goudy Old Style, one of the more than one hundred typefaces designed by Frederic William Goudy (1865–1947). Although Goudy began his career as a bookkeeper, he was so inspired by the appearance of several newly published books from the Kelmscott Press that he devoted the remainder of his life to typography in an attempt to bring a better understanding of the movement led by William Morris to the printers of the United States.

Produced in 1914, Goudy Old Style reflects the absorption of a generation of designers with things "ancient." Its smooth, even color combined with its generous curves and ample cut marks it as one of Goudy's finest achievements.

Composed by Creative Graphics,
Allentown, Pennsylvania

Printed and bound by Fairfield Graphics,
Fairfield, Pennsylvania

Designed by Cassandra J. Pappas

GLOVER

LIFE AND TIMES OF CAPTAIN N.

SARATOGA SPRINGS PUBLIC LIBRARY

SARATOGA SPRINGS PUBLIC LIBRARY

0 00 02 0128420 5